The li[illegible]ght came from fou[illegible]
had been placed on the grass amongst the [illegible] dogs. The wedges of yellow light lit up the statues, making them look beautiful and magical; their stony bodies appeared soft, as if they really were furry, and their stone eyes seemed to glint with life.

For several moments the dogs were all Bella saw, then a tall broad figure stepped forward from the shadows and entered the magical circle.

The figure had a man's body and legs, but his arms were not arms, but wings which he held wide open, spreading his magnificent feathers. But it was his head which was the worst. Bella trembled, looking at it, unable to tear her eyes from it.

The head of the man was that of a fish . . .

Also available by Rebecca Lisle,
and published by Yearling Books:

SHRUBBERY SKULDUGGERY

'A book to make you shiver with laughter
and fright at the same time'
Federation of Children's Book Groups, Pick of the Year

'A good rollicking story well told'
The Junior Bookshelf

'An excellent storyline'
Recent Children's Fiction

THE WEATHERSTONE ELEVEN

REBECCA LISLE

Illustrated by the author

YEARLING

For my husband
Keith Erskine

THE WEATHERSTONE ELEVEN
A YEARLING BOOK 0 440 86325 2

First published in Great Britain by Doubleday,
a division of Transworld Publishers Ltd

PRINTING HISTORY
Doubleday edition published 1992
Yearling edition published 1994
Reprinted 1994

Yearling Books are published by Transworld Publishers Ltd,
61–63 Uxbridge Road, Ealing, London W5 5SA,
in Australia by Transworld Publishers (Australia) Pty Ltd,
15–25 Helles Avenue, Moorebank, NSW 2170,
and in New Zealand by Transworld Publishers (NZ) Ltd,
3 William Pickering Drive, Albany, Auckland.

Set in Linotype Bembo by Chippendale Type Ltd

Printed and bound in Great Britain by
Cox & Wyman Ltd, Reading, Berkshire

Chapter One

Nothing seemed to stir in the Ancient History Museum except the drifting dots of dust illuminated by the early-morning sunshine as it streamed in through the high, small windows. But the building wasn't entirely empty – the night guard was there.

A secretive, peculiar man, he was rarely seen by any of the day staff. It was nearly time for him to go off duty, but he was taking one last look at his favourite exhibit, a man-eating fish with purple scales and bulbous eyes. He polished the display cabinet with his sleeve, checking there were no smudges, then went on his way to collect the morning post.

It was his last duty in the night shift and he liked it. Letters could be so rewarding: a child might have sent in cash for a badge or poster –

the money went straight into his pocket. There might be a private letter to one of the historians or the director worth steaming open – always a chance of blackmail there. And it was how, when he was working in the Egyptian Museum, he'd heard about the tomb of Katuom. He'd got there before the other scientists and plundered the tomb of some very fine treasures. But the dealers had cheated him of his money, as usual, and now he was on a different trail – looking for Merlin's dogs.

Suddenly the guard pounced on one particular letter. It was handwritten, marked PRIVATE and addressed to Mr Richard Bradberry – a mild, vague man who worked in the research department. The man checked the postmark: Cornwall. 'Ah, ha!' he whispered and, with trembling hands, carried it swiftly to the staff kitchen to steam it open.

He read its contents and his eyebrows rose, his smile broadened, and his goggly eyes bulged with glee. 'This is it, this is it!' he told himself and stifling his chuckles – though there were only the stuffed animals and fragments of pot to hear him – he picked up the phone and dialled.

'McGregor? McGregor is that you?'

'Aw, heck, hello? Who's this? Wassa time?'

'It's me, Boyle.'

'Who? Boil? Oh, Boyle, Boyle. Of course, yes, morning.'

'Are you awake? Listen carefully. I need some help with a little something down in Cornwall . . . Yeah, a bit like the job we did in Egypt but not so hot. I want you to book in at . . .' he read the address from the letter, '. . . Weatherstone Hall – it's some sort of guesthouse – and wait for me. You'll need a cover, can't be idle – hill walking, butterfly catching or something. OK?

Start snooping, find out all you can about . . .' he looked round nervously, and lowered his voice, '. . . about what's down there, and I'll join you soon. What? Yes, same pay as last time.'

Mr Boyle took one last look at the letter before he put it back, grinning all the while. He creased the letter up a bit, trod on it and smeared coffee across the back – 'Ah dear, the things the Post Office get up to,' he could hear himself explaining to the day guard when he handed it over.

Finally, he leaned back in his chair, smiling a nasty smile. 'It paid off!' he said to the bare walls. 'It paid off. Three months in this hole, every letter, every word watched and listened to, and now I have it! Sorry, Bradberry, you old duffer. The gold-seekers will be mine!' Closing his eyes, he recited from memory the old rhyme he'd seen and copied from Richard Bradberry's room:

'Come again, break from the past,
Throw off your gritty, stony cast.
Ye eleven magical dogs of old
As once for Merlin, now find me GOLD.'

Chapter Two

Mr Bradberry staggered into his house with his arms full of files, folders, magazines and unopened letters. He let them slither on to the kitchen table with a grateful sigh.

'Dad!' Arabella picked up the archaeologist's magazine, *Stones and Bones*, and peeled off the bread now stuck to its underside. 'Dad!'

'Sorry, Bella. Phew! How can I be expected to wade through all this lot *and* do my research!'

'Why not just put it all in the bin, darling?' It was Mrs Bradberry, or Fionella Bradberry-Fortesque as she was known to the fans of her romantic novels. 'It's all as dull as ditch-water, anyway . . . Had a busy day?'

'Yes, very. Had a good day working on *The Love That Lies Snoring*?'

'Richard! You know that's not what it's . . .'

'*Love Dies For Darning*?'

'Richard!'

'*A Dove Dies Farming*?'

'You know very well it's *Love Lies Burning* and yes, I've done a whole chapter today.'

'That must have been exhausting,' said Mr Bradberry, giving Bella a wink.

Bella grinned, but not so her mother could see, and started to sort the post into a pile. 'What on earth happened to this one?' She waved the crumpled, trodden-on envelope at her father. 'It says it's private. Pooh! And it smells awful, like rotten fish or something.'

'Oh, that's the one the Post Office mangled apparently. Here, let's have a look.'

Mr Bradberry opened it and began to read its contents. As he read he froze, his breathing seemed to stop and his eyes grew round with wonder and amazement.

'Richard! Richard, what on earth is it? Has somebody died? Have you won the pools?'

'By Jingo!' cried Mr Bradberry. 'Nothing like that, or rather yes, it could be the pools. It's about Merlin, at least it could be, I'm sure it could be!'

'Oh, no!' cried Bella and her mother in unison. 'Not *Merlin*!'

Mr Bradberry didn't notice.

'The letter's from a Mrs Gumm who lives in Cornwall and she's found some stone dogs, very old ones . . . apparently they were excavating to install new pipes at the guesthouse she owns – Weatherstone Hall – and they discovered ten stone dogs. Oh, bliss and blessings upon their dear heads, it must be them . . . And the best of it is, she hasn't told anyone else about it! I'm the only archaeologist who knows. She wants me to come down and investigate, see how old they are and if they really might be connected to Merlin.'

'You think everything's connected to Merlin,' said Bella. 'You'd have called me Merlin if you could.'

Mr Bradberry appeared not to hear.

'Remember that ancient rhyme I found?'

'How could we forget?' said Mrs Bradberry, wearily.

'I do,' said Bella. 'I remember it and it said

Merlin had eleven dogs. You said ten had been found in Cornwall.'

'Don't be a fuss-pot, Arabella. What's one dog here or there? It might still be buried, it might have got broken, it might . . . Yes, I'm sure these dogs might be Merlin's. Of course, there are historians who don't believe there were ever any dogs and certainly not that they could sniff out gold, but since I came across that ancient rhyme, I feel more strongly than ever . . .'

'What was it again?' asked Bella. 'How does it go?'

Mr Bradberry repeated the words:

> 'Come again, break from the past,
> Throw off your gritty, stony cast.
> Ye eleven magical dogs of old
> As once for Merlin, now find me GOLD.'

'It's nice,' said Bella thoughtfully. 'It does definitely say eleven though.'

'Don't be difficult, daughter. Well that's it then,' said Mr Bradberry. 'I'll phone her up and we'll go down on Saturday.'

'Saturday! But Dad, that's when we're going to Spain, you and me, don't you remember?'

'Spain can wait,' said Mr Bradberry. 'An

opportunity like this to maybe find Merlin's grave, to have proof the magic dogs existed, to be the first to see these dogs . . . Bella, such things just cannot wait.'

He went out, carrying his precious letter with him.

'Oh, Mum!'

'I know, it's a shame. If I'd have been coming we could have still gone, but you know I can't get away, not with the new book launch and everything – *Blind Passion*'s selling quite well, you know . . . Once Richard and I ended up in Kathmandu instead of a weekend in Robin Hood's Bay. It was great fun actually . . . You'll have a nice time in Cornwall, and at least I won't have to worry about you getting sunstroke, will I?'

Chapter Three

'I suppose it can't rain every day,' said Bella, staring out of the train window at the grey British countryside as it sped past.

'Oh I don't know,' said Mr Bradberry. 'I believe Cornwall can get anything up to ten centimetres of rain a day in the middle of summer.'

'You're teasing me . . . aren't you?'

Mr Bradberry grinned. 'Of course. We'll have a great time. Shame your mother couldn't come, she used to enjoy this sort of thing – before she became a writer, of course.'

'Tell me more about Merlin's dogs, Dad. If I know a bit I can be your assistant, can't I? Help you solve the puzzle.'

'Certainly you can help. Do you realize this is the first time you've shown any interest in my work, ever?'

'It's the thought of the gold,' said Bella, grinning. 'I want the dogs to find me gold like it says they did for Merlin.'

'Oh, goodness, forget about that! That's not important. I'm not interested in that bit; a great and eminent historian like myself expects to be poor . . .'

'Well, it might suit you but . . .'

They were interrupted by the carriage door opening suddenly and loudly. The rattle and roar of the engine filled the small room for a second as a man wearing a large hat poked his head in.

'Sorry!' he muttered into his scarf, which was wrapped round the lower half of his face. 'Sorry.' He backed out and closed the door with a bang.

Mr Bradberry shrugged.

'As I was saying, well, it's not the gold I'm after but Merlin himself. I've done a great deal of research on him . . . .'

'I know, Dad, how could I not know.'

'. . . and I and some other historians are sure he used a pack of golden-haired dogs – not just for hunting and tracking down enemies, but also for finding gold. Coming upon that ancient rhyme last month has made me even more sure.

Just think how useful it would be to have some animals like that around the house – even your mother would let you have one! There are so many clues, so many pointers to this, but no proof . . . Until now, until these dogs were found. They could be Merlin's. History has it that Merlin disappeared – on his own accord – and would come back when Britain needed him. People have been searching for that grave, that secret resting place, for centuries! And his dogs? Would he have left them behind? Would he have . . . Oh, blast it! There's that odd man again!'

'Where?' Arabella turned to the door.

'He's gone now. He was peering in at us. I do wish people wouldn't be so rude!'

'Go on, Dad, what about the dogs?'

'Yes, well, my point is, he wouldn't have left his magic dogs on earth for mere mortals to use, he would have either buried them with him or hidden them somewhere in some shape or form and what better than stone statues? That ancient rhyme suggests that one could break the spell or enchantment and so get the dogs to find gold again.'

'I thought you didn't want the gold!'

'I don't, I don't, but where the dogs are, so must Merlin be and if, just if, we could somehow get the dogs free from their stony state, surely they would lead us to Merlin, their master? And then surely, wouldn't I get a professorship for finding him? Hmmm?'

'Perhaps, but you seem to forget, there are only ten dogs.'

'Then, daughter dear, we must find the eleventh, mustn't we?'

Chapter Four

Mr Bradberry and Bella walked up the path from the village, struggling against the buffeting wind which tore at their hair and clothes. The air was damp and salty and seemed to coat them with a sticky, moist layer. To their left, the grey sea raged and roared, crashing against the rocks in white foam and then sucking away with a dragging sound. Above them towered Weatherstone Hall, stark and cold.

'This is fun, hey, Bella?' Mr Bradberry shouted.

Bella grinned back, too breathless to speak.

At last they stopped in front of the old house and gazed up at it in wonder. 'It's brilliant,' sighed Bella.

The house was built on the remains of an ancient castle, some of which still existed, though only as crumbling walls and leaning towers. Mounds of boulders and stones were green with ivy which crept up the walls of the house and over the roof. High walls on the left of the house protected an enclosed garden where they could just make out the tops of fruit trees tossing in the wind.

They approached the front door. The ornate brass knocker, shaped into a dog's head, crashed thunderously as Mr Bradberry hammered it against the door, sending flakes of paint flying off the chipped and scratched paintwork. The bang echoed inside the house as if it were an empty cave and was followed immediately by the deep, hollow barking of a dog.

The door opened.

'Hello, hello,' chirped a little woman, smiling up at them. She had round dark eyes like marinated olives and wore bright lipstick. 'The Bradberrys? Yes! Did you have a good journey? Left your bags at the station? Do come in out of the wind. Isn't it terrible?' She ushered them inside. 'Get back, Lady, back.' She pushed the black dog back along the stone-flagged corridor. 'She likes to check out all the visitors,' explained Mrs Gumm. 'She's quite safe, very gentle. Do come through.'

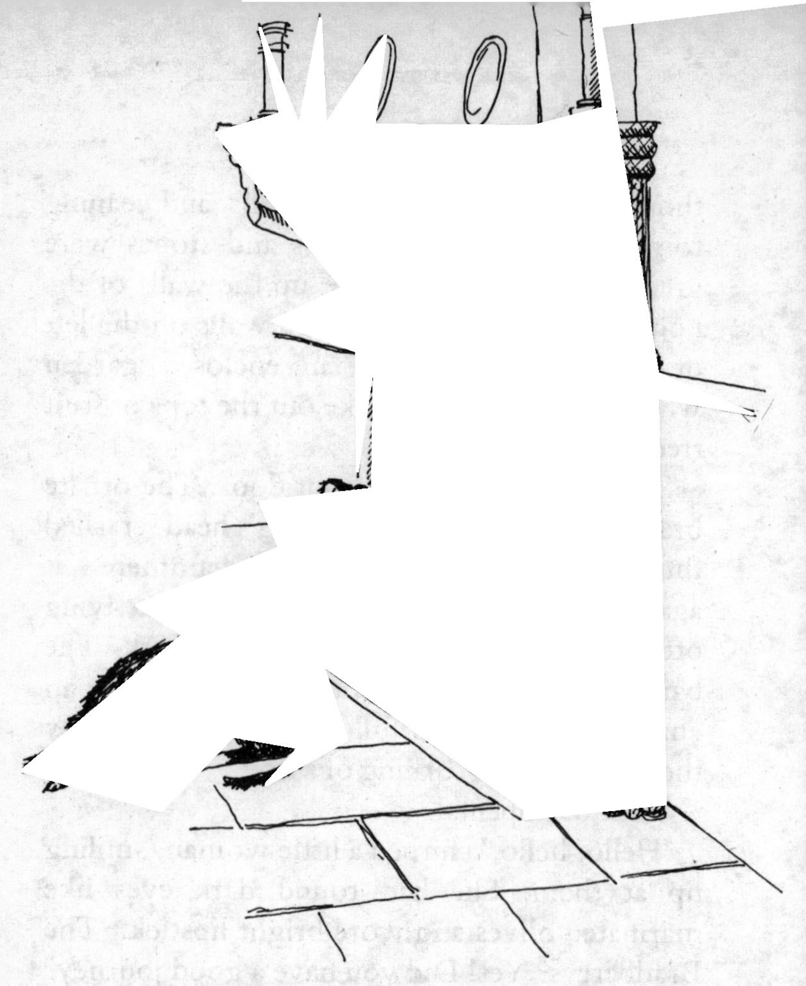

Mrs Gumm led them down the chilly corridor and into a vast hall which was hung with gigantic tapestries and dark glossy portraits. A fire crackled in the grate and Lady and another, older dog sat beside the hearth, basking in its warmth.

Bella went over to the dogs and stroked them.

'Oh, they're beautiful, specially Lady. Is the other dog old? She's all grey around the nose.'

'That's her mother. We always have the two female dogs here, it's a tradition going back generations so I believe. We always keep one dog from each litter.'

'So Lady's related to dogs that lived here years and years ago?' asked Arabella. 'She's got a sweet face. I'd love a dog but Mummy won't let me have one.'

'There, look, Lady's quite taken to you. That's very unusual,' said Mrs Gumm. 'She doesn't normally like our guests. Look, she's giving you her paw. Well, Billy will be annoyed.'

'Billy?'

'My boy. He's eight. He thinks Lady loves only him!' Mrs Gumm smiled. 'Now, come on upstairs and I'll show you to your rooms. I have some things to discuss with you, Mr Bradberry, and some papers to show you – but that can wait. I feel sure I can trust you with this archaeological find – you were most highly recommended – but it's been so hard . . . my husband's dead, you know, and not having anyone to turn to for advice . . .'

'Don't worry, Mrs Gumm, I shall do my very best for you,' said Mr Bradberry and, following her, they went up the stairs to their rooms.

When Mrs Gumm finally went downstairs again, Bella rushed into her father's bedroom which adjoined hers.

'Oh, Dad! A four-poster bed! I've always wanted one, and a desk with all those little pigeon-holes and drawers and things and oh, you've got a wonderful bed! And so many pictures – all of dogs! It's the most doggy place I've ever seen. Do you think it's anything to do with the stone dogs?'

Mr Bradberry sat on his bed then flopped down flat on the sagging mattress. Something went 'poing' beneath him.

'Oh, I don't think so,' he said. 'It's the Gumms that are dog-mad.' He yawned.

'It's got a fantastic feel to it, this place,' said Bella, going over to the window and looking out at the sea. 'It feels so friendly, it's as if I've been here before or known Mrs Gumm before or something. Do you know what I mean?'

'Mmm.'

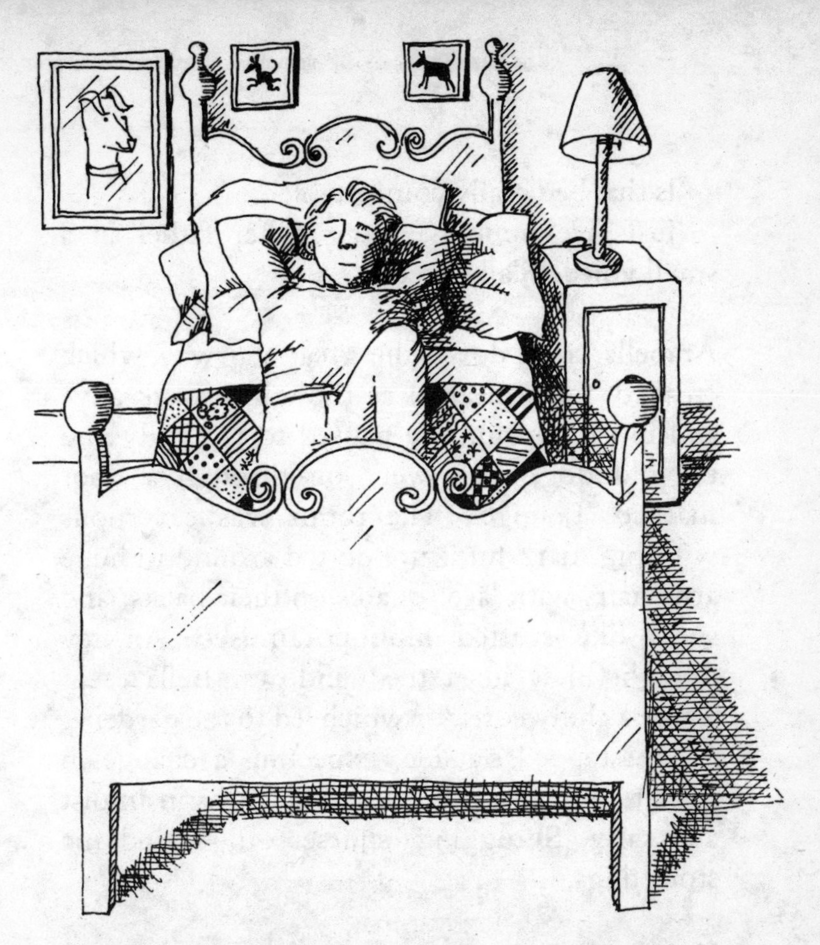

'The wind's dropped a bit. It's still pretty grey. Our bags aren't here yet, so shall we go out and explore? Dad?'

'Mmm?'

'Dad. What are you doing? Wake up! We're here to investigate. We're doing research, that's what you said!'

'Did I?' Mr Bradberry didn't open his eyes.

'Is that bed really comfortable?'

'Just five minutes,' begged her father in a small voice. 'S'all I need.'

Arabella crept down the great stairway which creaked and squeaked as though it were alive and in great pain. She paused to pat Lady and the old dog, then went on through a door marked 'Lounge'. The room was cavernous with big, dark furniture dotted around it: huge armchairs with lace squares on their backs, and sofas like stuffed hippopotamuses. An icy draught blew in at the windows. Bella crept down a chilly corridor which led to the garden.

She stepped outside, expecting a change in the air, but it was the same outside as in, moist and salty. Shrugging, she set off to find the stone dogs.

Chapter Five

The garden was blissfully sheltered from the sea wind, but it was not warm and Bella couldn't help momentarily wishing for the hot Spanish sun.

She was standing on a paved terrace with steps down to a square of lawn, beyond which and on both sides was a tangle of greenery. In the centre of the grass was a vast marble fountain but it was badly stained, dry and cracked. Looking more closely, Bella saw that the twisted stems of clematis and wisteria on the walls were being choked by vicious dark strands of ivy and that the beds were a mass of weeds, fighting the flowers for space and light.

She walked on down the stone path which became more and more cracked and covered with moss and grass. There were broken urns

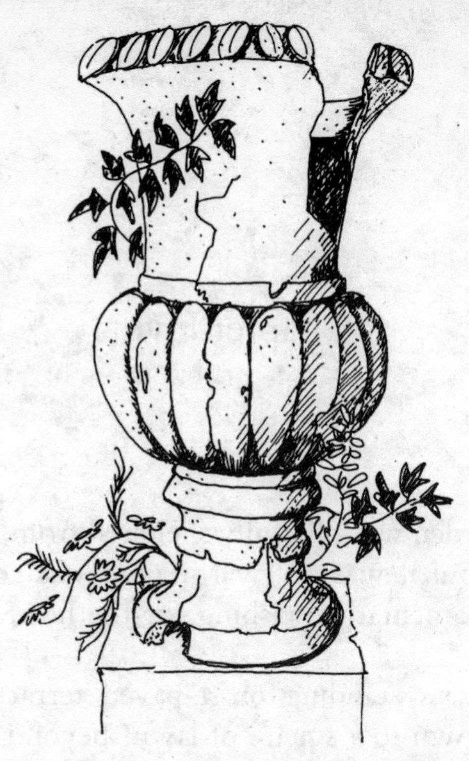

and ivy-covered statues; derelict sheds and a circular summerhouse with a young tree twisting right through its roof. Everywhere was a mass, a tangle, of fiercely growing vegetation.

At last the winding path led Bella to the orchard where apples already glistened redly and purple plums were dripping from the branches like fat beads on a necklace.

It was at the back of the orchard in a partly walled, bare patch of land that the stone dogs had been found. Pushing open the iron gate,

Bella seemed to step into another time and place as she saw, for the first time, the Weatherstone dogs.

Here, the grass was long and it rustled against her legs in the wind which swept over the low and broken wall. She felt suddenly nervous and glanced over her shoulder, but there was no-one there. She went nearer the gaping brown scar in the green grass and stared at the grey stone statues.

They were beautiful.

'Oh, lovely, lovely,' she crooned, weaving round their bodies, touching their gritty skins. 'You are Beauty and you are Blondine. This is Lydia and Rowena and Princess . . . And here

Claudine and Cylla, and that must be Morwena and . . .' She stroked the animal's sleek head, caressing its neck and shoulders, speaking their names without realizing it. 'I know you, I know you,' she whispered into the stone shell of an ear.

Then, suddenly, the magic was broken, and Bella straightened up, full of alarm, certain now that she *was* being watched. She looked all around, sensing rather than seeing danger. She caught the hint of a scent on the wind, the strong sea-smell of fish, old and bitter and . . . horrid. Bella turned and ran.

As she ran it seemed as though she was running as easily and swiftly as a dog, for her feet seemed hardly to touch the ground. She thought she glimpsed shadows racing along beside her; she heard the rush of bodies running in the wind and smelt strange, strong animal smells and felt the warmth of close bodies, as if, for a few seconds, she was amongst a living, breathing mass of animals. Then it was gone. She fell into the calm greenery of the orchard and rolled on to the grass.

She lay still, closed her eyes and tried to calm her racing heart. She'd panicked, that was all. It was the strange, bleak field and the wind and

. . . She opened her eyes. She was all alone and there was nothing to fear from the garden.

'Arabella Bradberry, you are an idiot,' she told herself sharply and, picking herself up, she went back to the house.

Chapter Six

Bella found her father in what was called The Garden Room, having tea with a small boy.

'We saw you coming up the path,' said her father. 'Had a good time? Sorry I fell asleep. This is Billy, by the way.'

Billy had spiky hair and a spiky nose. His round, bright eyes were just like Mrs Gumm's.

'This is my daughter, Arabella. Bella, Billy Gumm.'

'Crikey, what a dreadful name,' said Billy, grinning at her. 'Who landed you with that stinker?'

'I did, Billy,' said Mr Bradberry.

'Oh, crikey . . .'

'Anyway, I think Billy Gumm's worse. I hope your middle name doesn't begin with a Y.'

Billy looked puzzled. 'Why?' he asked.

'Because then you'd be B Y Gumm – By Gum!'

'Oh.' Billy looked worried. 'I hope Bigsey Wilcox at school never thinks of that one,' he said. 'He'd love it. Here, have some tea.' Billy thrust a cup and saucer into her hand. 'Like the china?'

The cup he had given her seemed alive with a trellis of brilliant blue flowers while the saucer was dappled with orange, pink and gold dots.

'It's wonderful.'

'Here, grab hold of this.' He gave her a red and white striped plate in the centre of which were gold initials. Bella didn't have time to read them before Billy had dumped a peanut butter sandwich, a crumpet and a jam-filled bun on to it.

Bella staggered back into a chair and began eating: the sea air had made her hungry.

'It's very interesting china,' said Bella, between mouthfuls.

The table was piled high with the extraordinary collection. Almost no two pieces were the same, and the colours so bounced and clashed against each other that Bella was surprised she couldn't hear them.

'All this lovely food, Billy,' said Mr Bradberry. 'Isn't anyone else coming to eat?'

'Nah, not now. That Darren McGregor's already been in and eaten ten people's share – and he's thinner than a piece of string! Don't know how he does it. He says painting gives him an appetite but he doesn't do much that I can see.'

'Is he another guest?'

'Yes. We've got some odd bods at the moment.'

'Ourselves included?' asked Mr Bradberry.

'I should say so,' said Billy, then went red, choked and stuttered: 'I mean, no, no, of course not.'

'I've been to look at the stone dogs, Daddy,' said Bella. 'They're brilliant. They're lovely! So life-like that I really felt they *were* alive – no, that's not quite right. I mean, I felt they could be alive – oh, it's hard to explain, but I thought they were magical. You should have come and seen them.'

'I hope they're very, very old,' said Billy, 'and very, very valuable. We need the money.'

'Well then, so do I – hope so, I mean,' said Mr Bradberry. 'Would you show Bella round a little, Billy? I need to speak to your mother about what I shall be doing here.'

Billy looked shyly at Arabella.

'If she wants,' he said.

'I suppose it would be OK,' said Bella, pretending not to care. They said goodbye to Mr Bradberry and set off through the garden again.

'I've just thought,' said Bella. 'If your first name was Edward, you'd be . . .'

'E By Gum,' said Billy, glumly. 'I was rather hoping you wouldn't think of that. Come on, before you have another brain wave.'

They stepped out of a gate in the walled garden which led out to the front of the house. The wind had dropped and a pale, low-lying sun was just beginning to break through the clouds. All around the blue sea glinted as specks of sun hit it, blue, green and turquoise.

'It's fantastic,' said Bella.

'It'll be a lovely day tomorrow,' said Billy, looking up at the pink and grey sky. 'You'll be able to go on the beach, even swim, maybe.'

'I'll believe that when I'm doing it,' said Bella, shivering in the cool sea air. 'Let's hurry. Where are we going?'

'I thought you'd like to see the bay,' said Billy, leading her down the path towards the sea, 'and the bits of castle and the caves . . .'

'Caves? Oh, what caves?'

'These cliffs are riddled with them. Look over there,' and he pointed across the bay to where holes showed like black eyes in the distant cliff face. 'The caves and the old castle remains bring lots of archaeologists like your father. My uncle once believed Merlin had lived here too.'

'There's someone down there,' Bella interrupted. She pointed down to some large grey rocks where the water swirled white and frothy.

'Who is it?' asked Bella. 'Let's go and see what they're up to.'

They crept through the thin, bent trees and huddled down behind a big boulder to spy on the figure below.

'Oh, it's just Miss Longparish,' said Billy. 'No-one exciting. She's another guest. She fishes all the time.'

Miss Longparish appeared to be having a lot of difficulty with her apparatus. One rod was caught between her legs and another, together with a large net, had become lodged between the rocks. Miss Longparish fought them bravely, eventually ending up in a heap inside her fishing basket.

'She doesn't seem to know a lot about it,' said Billy. 'Oh,' he added, 'what on earth . . .'

Miss Longparish had finally freed herself and now she took out a large dead fish from her basket and fixed it on to the end of her line. Looking round quickly, she then flung the fish and line out into the water, propped up her rod and settled down in the hollow of a boulder to read her book.

Arabella and Billy exchanged a look.

'Very fishy,' said Billy.

'It's fishing backwards. She must be mad.'

'I think most of our guests usually are.'

'Except for us,' Bella corrected him.

'Of course, except for you.'

'She may be mad,' said Bella, 'or of course she may be very clever and just be pretending to be an angler to throw us off the scent.'

'What scent?'

'Merlin's scent. Why is she here? Not to fish, so why not to investigate the stone dogs? Hah, I bet I'm right! I must tell Dad – he trusts everyone and goodness knows what secrets he might give away! Come on. I'm cold. Let's get back.'

The short wiry grass was criss-crossed with tiny footpaths, some made by tourists and others by animals. Here and there were scrubby bushes and large boulders and patches of bramble and wild flowers.

Bella led the way. As they walked, she told

Billy everything she had learned about Merlin and his gold-seeking dogs. They hardly looked around and so were both surprised when they reached a side entrance to the house, where a crumbling arch dripping ivy and white roses like cake decorations led into a large courtyard.

'How did I get here?' asked Bella.

'You were leading. I thought maybe you'd come this way before.'

'No, no, it was really odd, Billy, I did it automatically. I wasn't thinking at all and my feet just came along that little track and here we are and – where's the fountain?'

Bella stepped across the cobbled courtyard towards the centre.

'There used to be a fountain,' she told Billy. 'It had a marble dolphin which spouted water.'

'Well, I never saw it,' said Billy, scratching his head. 'Though there probably was, you can see a pattern in the cobbles where big stones were, but . . .'

'And over here,' Bella went on, walking across to a door, 'once upon a time was . . .'

But she was interrupted by a shout and a sudden loud TWANG!, followed by a whooshing noise as an arrow flew through the air, straight towards her.

Chapter Seven

The arrow curved in the air, landing with a nutty plonk right in a patch of earth at her feet. It quivered there like a plucked guitar string.

Sitting astride the broken wall, Bella now saw, was a thin, grey-haired man. He had long fluffy hair standing out around his head like a dandelion clock, and a brown bony face.

In his hands, but no longer pointing directly at her, was the bow and arrow.

'Hey,' said Arabella. 'You nearly hit me.'

'Goodness me,' said the old man. He seemed very flustered and surprised. 'What have I done? Everything went blurred and I thought I saw a knight in armour . . . Ridiculous!'

Arabella shivered. For her, too, the courtyard had been a blurred image, as if she was seeing it as it was now and, overlying that, another picture of how it had once been.

'Just over there,' said Bella, pointing to a gaping hole in the wall where trees and bushes peeped through, 'there was a door which went up to a little room where somebody – somebody famous – used to work. Oh, what am I saying?'

Billy came towards them.

'You're both bonkers,' he said, crossly.

'Really, Uncle Jack, you must be careful with that bow and arrow. It's lethal and you nearly hit Bella, and I think you've probably done her some terrible mental damage. She's a guest too. Come on, Bella, let's go inside.'

He turned her round and led her back into the house.

'Uncle Jack's a bit – you know,' he explained. 'He had a great disappointment when he was young and he's never been quite the same since. He's a great chap, really.'

'What was he disappointed by?'

'What do you think?' said Billy, scornfully. 'A girl!'

At dinner that evening, Bella had a chance to see the other guests.

There were two ancient old ladies, very fragile-looking, like porcelain figures that really belonged on a mantelpiece. They were sisters called Miss Agnes and Miss Nellie Silver.

'They've been here many times,' Mrs Gumm said quietly to the Bradberrys, then much more loudly to one of the sisters: 'You come here a lot, don't you, Miss Silver?'

'We've been here eleven times and it's always lovely,' said one sister.

'The sea's lovely,' quavered the other sister.

'The cliffs are lovely,' said the first, 'and the sea.'

'So is the grass. Lovely.'

They smiled vaguely at Arabella, as if she, perhaps, had never seen or heard of the sea or the grass. Batty, Bella thought, totally batty . . . or were they? She peered at them, wondering if perhaps they, too, were here to uncover the mystery of the stone dogs.

Bella tore her gaze away from the two Miss Silvers, to be introduced to Mr McGregor.

'Darren McGregor, our artist.'

Bella and her father shook hands politely. He doesn't look like an artist to me, Bella thought. He had short, inartistic fingers and thin, mousy, inartistic hair. He could have been any age between twenty and forty, with a rather grey, pale complexion, as if he lived under a stone. Or, Bella imagined, looking at his crumpled jacket and creased trousers, he'd been packed away into a suitcase while he was still damp and never ironed. He smelled like that too.

'Miss Longparish isn't down yet,' said Mrs Gumm, looking round the dining-room. 'That's her table in the corner, and of course there's Mr Boyle yet to come. Ah, here's . . .'

A door opened and the waiter came in.

'That's the one that nearly shot me!' Bella whispered loudly to her father. 'The one with the bow and arrow. The waiter.'

'Oh, really Uncle Jack,' said Mrs Gumm, who had overheard her. 'Not again!'

The waiter, looking a little sheepish, swept smoothly round the table as if he were on roller skates and flourished a napkin at Bella.

'My dear girl!' he exclaimed. 'Delighted to meet you again! Hope you have forgiven me. So stupid. Lovely dinner tonight. I cooked it. Do you like mushrooms?'

'Mushrooms?'

'Yes. Get our own mushrooms right here. So damp – grow them on the walls . . .' He grinned at her astonished face. 'Just pick them off. Eat them. Mushrooms!' He glided out again, chuckling at his own joke.

'There's a lot of it about here,' Bella whispered to her father. 'Hope it's not catching.'

'What's that dear?'

'Madness.'

They sat down at their allotted table beside the window just as Miss Longparish came in.

Arabella would not have recognized her from the person she'd seen on the rocks as she was swathed in gauze-like scarves which so covered her face and shoulders that she was hardly visible. She came over to the Bradberrys' table and introduced herself.

'Lovely fishing here,' she said in a very quiet voice. 'Bass. Sea bass. Hope you enjoy your stay.'

Bella could just make out a heart-shaped face with pale lips and pale blue eyes beneath the veil. She was quite old, at least sixty, and didn't look in the least like a fisherwoman.

'That's the one I told you about,' hissed Bella to her father. 'Very odd behaviour. Disguised, I bet. Don't tell her any of your secrets.'

'Bella, don't be ridiculous, she's just here for the fishing. I can't go around suspecting everyone of being here for the same reason as me!'

Just then, the door opened and the final guest at Weatherstone Hall came in.

Chapter Eight

The new arrival greeted the other guests before he came over to Bella's table, so she had several moments to observe him secretly.

She stared at him, sure she'd seen him somewhere before, and the more she stared, the less she liked what she saw. He was a big man, with broad shoulders and a big head. His eyes protruded and this, together with his rather shiny skin, made him look like a squidgy amphibian. He had dark grey hair which was thin at the front of his head and long, tied in a straggly ponytail, at the back. He turned towards their table and Bella felt herself blush and look away.

'Mr Bradberry, how do you do,' he said, shaking her father's hand, which Mr Bradberry immediately and stealthily wiped on his trouser leg. 'My name is Sidney Boyle.'

'Have we met before?'

'I don't think so, Mr Bradberry. It's not very likely. I travel abroad a great deal. I trade, buy things here and sell things there.'

'I see, but I'm sure I've seen you somewhere . . .' Mr Bradberry sniffed uneasily. 'Is it fish tonight, Bella?'

Mr Boyle seemed relieved to go and, taking this as his cue, he backed away to his table.

Mr Boyle walked strangely, almost as though he were lopsided, thought Bella, watching his retreating back. His left hand was thrust deep into his pocket, making a big, solid lump – or was it just his hand? Bella peered round her father, trying to see. There was something else inside his pocket, something round and feathery. She was sure it was feathery. A bird? Had he got a bird stuffed in there? Suddenly, she noticed Darren McGregor watching her with his little pale eyes and she straightened up and looked away.

She was going to have to be very careful here. Things, people, *everything* was not what it seemed.

The following day, which was bright and sunny just as Billy had promised, Bella and her father went to see the stone dogs.

Bella led the way and when they reached a spot where the dogs were visible, Mr Bradberry stopped, froze and stared.

'All right, Dad?'

'Just brilliant, Bella.' Mr Bradberry sighed deeply and strode towards the statues. 'Brilliant, brilliant, brilliant . . . as you might say.'

He began to walk round the stone dogs, peering at them first through his glasses, then more closely without them.

'Mrs Gumm's worried they'll be stolen, but look at them! Heavy great things, you'd need a crane. Oh, these are wonderful and the right age – must be five hundred AD. Goodness, how fantastic and wonderful!'

'What are you going to do now?'

'Measure them. Draw them. Make notes. Photograph them.'

'Take one of me,' said Bella, slipping in between two of the dogs. 'Here, between Rowena and Princess.'

Mr Bradberry stopped still, looking at her sharply.

'What was that you said?'

'Would you photograph me with the dogs?'

'But you gave them names.'

'Yes, Rowena and Princess, and these are Cylla and Claudine and Pandora and Griselda.'

'Arabella Bradberry, what are you talking about? How do you know these dogs' names?'

'Because . . . because . . .' The answer had

been on the tip of her tongue, but now it had gone. She frowned, confused. 'I just do. I did as soon as I saw them.'

Mr Bradberry was eyeing her suspiciously. 'You're teasing me!'

'No, really.'

'Which one is that?' He pointed to one of the dogs.

'Lydia.'

'And this one?'

'Beauty.'

'Just a minute . . .' Mr Bradberry knelt down beside Beauty and peered at the collar around her neck. Hanging from it was a round medallion with some letters carved into the stone. He rubbed and blew at the inscription which was encrusted with earth and bits of moss.

'Bea-u-ty,' he read out slowly. 'Beauty. Ah, so that's how you did it. Well done, you really had me fooled, Bella.'

'But, but Dad, I never saw those before.' She went over to Morwena and found she could just make out the ancient letters in the dog's name tag. 'Yes, it says Morwena,' she agreed, 'but I knew before. I did, really and truly.'

'You are not a girl to tell lies, Bella,' he said

kindly, 'but on this occasion I think perhaps you were, well, imagining a lot.'

'I know these dogs, Daddy, I really do *know* them.'

'Hmm, well, my dear, tell me, if you know them so well, the name and whereabouts of the missing dog. Then I will believe you, really I will.'

Bella sighed.

'It's odd,' she said. 'I should know its name but I don't. I feel as if I used to, as if I knew it as well as my own. You know what it's like when you forget your own phone number? Just like that. But I don't know where she is, I wish I did.'

'But it's a she, is it?'

'Of course, they all are.'

'I shall check. Oh, they are truly wonderful, aren't they? Just imagine them alive. It's not hard, is it, with those expressions and the set of their heads? Imagine Merlin sending them off to dig for buried treasure, perhaps to steal for him or even fight for him. They would have been so powerful, such a fantastic weapon!'

'And they would have been brave and kind too,' said Bella. 'You can tell. I bet they looked after King Arthur and protected him.'

'Perhaps. It's all imagining. I must get on with my research and prove it.'

'It would be a pretty bad thing if an evil person got their hands on the eleventh dog first, wouldn't it?' said Bella, after a while. She was lying on the grassy bank, watching her father at work. Up towards the house, where the walls were crumbling, she spotted Mr McGregor setting up his easel and paints.

'Evil?'

'If someone bad found the eleventh dog and got the dogs alive again, like the rhyme says, then he'd be able to use them for bad things, wouldn't he?'

'I suppose so. But you forget, Bella, I'm the only person who knows about the rhyme *and* these dogs. Only me. Lots of historians know about the rhyme and probably lots of locals know about the dogs, but it's putting the two together that brings sense to it.'

'Hmm,' said Bella and she settled down to wait again, keeping a constant watch on the distant figure of Darren McGregor.

An hour later, they set off back to the Hall.

Mr Bradberry patted his notebook where it lay safely in his pocket. 'I'm sure I shall get something from this. I must talk to Mrs Gumm about where exactly the dogs were found. It may be that the eleventh is there too, perhaps thrown to one side or deeper. We must find that missing dog!'

'Let's go see what the artist is up to,' Bella suggested as they neared Mr McGregor, who was apparently painting the sea. But by the time they got close, Mr McGregor had begun packing his things up, and, as they reached his side, he was putting his final canvas into a large black folder.

'All finished for the day?' asked Mr Bradberry.

'Oh, hello there, didn't see you coming,' said Mr McGregor. 'Yes, I've finished. It's going well.'

Arabella looked at him suspiciously. There wasn't a single smudge of paint on his fingers or the faintest whiff of turpentine.

'Who's your favourite painter?' Bella asked him.

'Er, er, well.' Mr McGregor rubbed his nose and pulled at his large ear nervously. 'Oh, well, I like Picasso. Do you take much interest in the arts, Mr Bradberry?'

'I expect you like Dylan Hockney,' Bella put

in quickly, hoping her father wouldn't correct her.

'Ah, yes, our Dylan, lovely colours, don't you think, Mr Bradberry?'

Mr Bradberry tried not to smile as he nodded his agreement.

'And Constable?' Bella chimed in again.

'Police Constable? Where?' Mr McGregor spun round, eyes wide with alarm.

'She means the painter,' said Mr Bradberry.

'Of course, quite so, quite,' said Mr McGregor, sighing deeply. 'Constable, of course. Modern, yes. Oh dear, it is hot, isn't it?'

Arabella smiled smugly. She had been quite right in suspecting he wasn't an artist at all.

They parted company in the stone-flagged hall.

'Terribly hungry after all that work,' said Mr McGregor sheepishly. 'Sorry, must go and get some lunch.' He stowed his painting gear behind a chair and hurried off.

'Greed is a terrible thing,' said Bella, going over to the abandoned painting equipment. 'Cheating and lying probably have something to do with it . . .'

She began to unzip the black folder and take out the paintings.

'Bella! Bella, stop that immediately!' But even as her father spoke, he came over to look too.

'There! Look at that,' said Bella. 'I thought so! He wasn't painting the view at all – it's a rotten bowl of fruit!'

'Mm,' said Mr Bradberry thoughtfully. He dabbed his finger at the painting then stared at his clean fingertip: 'And he wasn't painting *that*, either.'

Father and daughter exchanged a look.

'So what exactly was he doing?' asked Bella. 'Be careful, Dad, I don't like the look of this at all.'

Chapter Nine

'I know you think you're the only one interested in the dogs,' Bella said to her father after lunch that day, 'but I don't. All the guests seem mighty suspicious to me. Please, just for me, will you keep your notes in the secret drawer of my desk?'

'Ridiculous child! Who are you suspicious of? Silly McGregor? He may not be a painter, but he's harmless. As I said, someone would need both the dogs and the rhyme to be a threat. And who else would be interested in finding Merlin?'

'Or interested in finding gold, Dad, don't forget.'

Mr Bradberry frowned, then nodded in agreement. 'There's something in that,' he said. 'All right, we'll hide the notes.'

Exploring the old wooden desk earlier, Bella

had discovered a secret drawer. It had no handle and could only be opened by pulling a tiny brass lever hidden inside another drawer.

'It only took you three seconds to find and open it, Bella,' said Mr Bradberry as he squeezed a bundle of tiny sheets of paper inside, 'so how long would it take a determined burglar?'

'Oh, ages if they were grown up,' said Bella confidently. 'You need a child's brain to find the way in there.'

'I hope you're right. What plans have you for this afternoon?'

'Billy's going to show me things – the caves maybe.'

'Caves? Don't go wandering in caves, Bella, it's easy to get lost. Never go so far inside that you can't see the entrance when you look back.'

'I promise.'

'And make sure Billy looks after you. Now, I must get on with my work. See you at teatime,' and Mr Bradberry settled down to his papers and calculations.

Arabella went down to the hall to wait for Billy. The two dogs were curled up in front of the fire as usual, but Lady stretched and got up to talk to Bella. Bella rubbed her ears and stroked her sleek head.

'Lady doesn't like other people.' It was Billy.

'I'm not other people,' said Bella. 'We're friends. I love her.'

'Humph,' said Billy. He patted his leg and called for Lady to come to him, but she stayed beside Bella, her nose pressed into Bella's leg. 'Lady! Lady!' he said sharply, but Lady only wagged her tail.

'I found out all about that thin artist today,' said Bella.

'Oh, yeah?' Billy tried not to let his hurt show: Lady had never, never done this before.

'He's not an artist, Billy.'

'So what?'

'He's so much *not* an artist that he's never even heard of David Hockney. I bet he's so much not an artist he doesn't even know which end of the brush to hold.'

Billy couldn't help grinning.

'But why pretend?' he said. 'It's very odd. Why should he need to? Hey, I've just seen him sneaking out into the garden. Shall we follow him and see what he's up to?'

Bella nodded.

'Come on then, we'd better hurry. Come on,

Lady, walkies!' This time Lady obediently followed them outside. 'D'you think he could be an archaeologist too? After the secret of the stone dogs?'

'He must be, but he doesn't seem clever enough for anything difficult like that. In fact, I would have said he was too dim to have thought of being disguised as an artist, but we'll see.'

They stood on the raised stone terrace in the walled garden, scanning the greenery.

'There he goes!' cried Billy, spotting McGregor's head above the bushes. 'Pity Lady's not a bloodhound . . . Let's go!'

They sped after McGregor, weaving along the twisting, overgrown paths as fast as they could. They soon found themselves just a few steps behind him and slowing down, crouched amongst the bushes. From the safety of the shrubbery they watched him disappear into the old broken summerhouse.

'What's he doing in there?'

'Let's creep round the back and have a look. There's a window round the other side. Quietly, or he'll hear.'

Lady wasn't interested in being quiet and spying on people; she wagged her tail and went

bounding off down the path in the opposite direction.

Carefully, the children sneaked round the little house, keeping their heads down and being as quiet as possible. As they drew nearer to the back of the building, and the broken window, they were startled to hear voices. Exchanging a surprised look they settled down under the cover of the overhead leaves, to listen.

'. . . so I got down here on the Thursday, like you said, and I've been out "painting" every day.' It was Darren McGregor.

'Yes, yes,' said the other man's voice, 'but have you found anything out? That's what you're paid to do. What were Bradberry and the girl up to this morning? Did they move the dogs? Did they touch them at all?'

Bella crouched lower in her hiding place. So McGregor had been spying on them, had he? How horrid!

Billy grinned at her and whispered, 'Recognize the voice? It's that awful old Boyle.'

'Shh!'

'They did a lot of talking and walking about and measuring, as far as I could see. Nothing interesting. Possibly that girl guessed I wasn't a real artist, but I don't think so.'

'Don't worry about her.'

'What about you, gov?' said McGregor. 'You're looking a bit seedy, if you don't mind me saying, and last night your hand was . . .'

'You noticed, did you? Look!'

There was movement inside the shed. Apparently, Mr Boyle was showing McGregor his hand, but the children could only guess at what it looked like.

'Cor look at that!' said McGregor. 'That's a thing, that is. Is that what's left from what that old Egyptian taught you – that Egyptian that helped us rob the tombs?'

'That's it. That was a good haul, wasn't it? But the Egyptian's magic wasn't so good. Remember how it was at the beginning? I could turn into a bird, fish or snake – easy as pie. The Egyptian never mentioned this . . . I hardly dare use it now.'

'I don't blame you, it's pretty revolting, boss,' agreed Darren. 'Er, I mean, yeah. Er, is that a bird bit or a fish bit?'

'Both.'

'Cor!'

'I tried it a couple of times, just for a spot of small-time stealing, and it was all right but then bits of me started turning, like now, and I can't get them back. Can't control it.'

'You best not try and use it at all then,' said McGregor.

'But I shall need it here. And this'll be the last time – just to help me find the missing dog. When this is over and I've restocked my bank account, I'll take a trip back to Egypt and pay that old wizard back for this.'

'Good idea.'

'We've got to get that dog before Bradberry does and break the spell that keeps them stone. We'll be rich, and I won't need to hang around old museums or turn into smelly animals to get what I want. Where's Bradberry right now?'

'Working in the library.'

'And the kids?'

'Er, well, I'm not sure, boss.'

'Check them out. There's something about that girl, the way she looks at me . . . it unnerves me. No wonder I'm not well. Drat that Egyptian!'

'Anything else, boss?'

'No. Just get on with spying . . . Oh, I see . . . Always the same with you, isn't it, McGregor? The open hand. Here you are then.'

The children heard the shuffle of paper money and felt, rather than saw, the way McGregor greedily stuffed the wad of notes into his pocket.

There were footsteps, the rustle of leaves, and finally silence as the two men disappeared.

'Phew!'

The two children let out their breath in one long, relieved sigh.

'Billy, did you hear them? What d'you think it meant? Oh, how awful! McGregor is helping

Boyle, and gosh, what do you think about Boyle? Did you understand about this Egyptian? Whatever he did to Boyle it doesn't work properly and now he's ill. How horrible! How horrible!'

'What do you think his hand looked like?'

'I never want to know.' Bella shuddered. 'Boyle sounded so cold and determined. I think they'd truly stop at nothing to get that missing dog. Oh, I must warn my father.'

'So you must. And we must keep a close watch on them. Your dad has got to find the missing dog first, break the spell and find Merlin. Otherwise, if that horrid Boyle does, he'll use the dogs himself for goodness knows what ghastly things, *and* get all the gold! Oh, Bella, I hope we can beat him!'

Chapter Ten

On the way back to the house they bumped into Uncle Jack who was just packing up his bows and arrows after some shooting practice.

'Arabella!' he cried when he saw her. 'A million apologies. My dear niece-in-law, the delightful Mrs Gumm to you, has insisted I make amends for trying to spear you with my arrow. Actually, had I really wanted to, you would not be standing here today. Come and have some lemonade.'

'Oh, well, thank you,' said Bella. 'We've just been . . .' But Billy gave her such a rough nudge that she stopped.

'Yes?'

'Nothing. Lemonade would be lovely.'

When Uncle Jack wasn't cooking or being a waiter, he could be found in the small room with large glass doors just below the steps at the back of the Hall. In the centre of the room was a large roll-top desk on which were scattered papers, plant pots, seed packets, pens, chocolates, feathers, a handful of broken pottery fragments and a couple of arrows. The desk took up a great deal of the space. There was an old three-legged oil stove, bags of coconut-fibre compost, an over-stuffed armchair into which four or maybe five cats were squashed, and an old record player beside which stacks of dusty, brittle old records, like tiny towers of Pisa, leaned and swayed.

On all the available wall-space were hundreds of pictures from magazines and black and white photographs, stuck higgledy-piggledy, layer upon layer. In the same way, the floor was layered with different pieces of carpet, making it nicely springy and soft under foot, like a good lawn.

'Ooo! What a lovely room,' Arabella breathed in delight. She immediately began to feel better and sank down happily amongst the cats.

'I *was* going to start some work on the garden,' said Uncle Jack, pouring them fresh lemonade. He looked bemused, as though he

couldn't understand why he hadn't. 'But I got carried away with . . . I don't know . . . I don't seem to have the drive these days.'

'It must have been a fantastic, beautiful garden once,' said Bella.

'A jolly long time ago,' said Billy, quietly.

'Oh, it was, it was,' agreed Uncle Jack. 'We had roses the size of footballs. Sweetpeas climbing higher than the house. We had hollyhocks and verbena, veronica and geraniums and clematis. Ah dear, clematis . . . You see, I just can't do it. I start, and I think I can forget and then I hear something like clematis and it takes me straight there . . . clematis to Clementine. One simple step. Clementine, my dear one.'

'Is that a flower too?'

'In a way, my dear, in a way.'

Bella looked at Billy for help, but he was just grinning so she shrugged and trying to change the subject, pointed to one of the photographs on the wall.

'Is this you, Uncle Jack?'

The picture showed a young couple, a thin young man with blond hair that floated like dandelion fluff around his head and, lounging against his side, a young woman holding a bunch of daisies.

'Ah ha,' Uncle Jack nodded in confirmation. 'Me and her. Clementine.'

'Oh, your flower? I see.' Bella began to understand. Hadn't Billy mentioned a great disappointment? A girl? 'I thought I recognized her just for a moment,' Bella went on. 'She wasn't famous, was she?'

'She should have been. She was the most beautiful woman in the world and the most clumsy.' He chuckled. 'Oh my darling . . . Put the record on for me, will you, Bill?'

Uncle Jack had sunk into a chair, and propping

his elbows on the desk, he gazed, dewy-eyed, at the photograph.

Billy obediently swung the needle across on the old gramophone and the record spun round with a scratchy cry. Uncle Jack closed his eyes as the first few bars of 'Clementine' filled the little room.

'Oh my darling, oh my darling, oh my darling, Clementine.' Uncle Jack and the voice on the record sang together, rising in a mournful wail and trailing off again with a sigh.

'Never even said goodbye,' said Uncle Jack, speaking to the photograph. 'Not a note, not a word. Nothing left except that darling statue. Darling Clementine.'

Arabella suddenly felt a second sharp nudge in her back; it was Billy. He beckoned her to come out. She eased the cats from her lap and tiptoed out into the garden again, not daring even to say goodbye to Uncle Jack, who seemed deep in his dreams.

'Honestly!' cried Billy, when they were safely outside. 'Sometimes I think he's gone soft in the head!'

'He's not soft. It's just love. What statue does he mean? Were they going to get married then? What happened?'

'I don't know. Don't ask *me*. Can't someone just change their minds if they want to? Or perhaps she jumped into the sea and swam to America. Maybe she was kidnapped by pirates. I don't know!'

'It's tragic, Billy, you shouldn't joke.'

'If she could muck up his life like this by *not* being here, imagine what she'd have done if she *was* here! Good riddance, I say!'

'You grown-ups are funny things,' Bella told her father that evening.

'Why, dear?'

'Because I've just told you the most incredible story about Mr Boyle and his hand and how an old Egyptian taught him magic to turn into animals and how he's after the missing stone dog too, and you're still sitting there reading.'

'Mmm.'

'Dad, you do believe me don't you?'

Mr Bradberry put down his book, *Statistical Mathematics for Archaeological Time Spans*, and looked up at Bella.

'I sort of believe you,' he said, eyeing her carefully.

'Sort of? What does that mean?'

'Well, Bella, did you *see* Mr Boyle?'

'No.'

'You just heard what you thought was his voice?'

'Yes.'

'And then he said his hand had turned into a bird or something?'

'McGregor looked at it and said yuk, how horrid it was, and Boyle said it was part-bird and part-fish . . .'

'And did you see his hand?'

'No, but . . .'

'And did you see Mr Boyle hand over money?'

'No.'

Father and daughter stared at each other.

'But you want proof,' said Bella, glumly, 'even though you know as well as I do that Boyle is a baddie. It's written all over him. Why else would he and McGregor be here? They're after the dogs too. They want the dogs to find them gold. Why don't you believe me?'

'I said I sort of believe you,' said Mr Bradberry, 'and I do. But, as you say, I want proof. However, I shall certainly take care, yes, and you must too, Bella. And tonight, let's have a good look at Boyle and his hidden hand, shall we?'

At dinner time, Bella watched the door anxiously, waiting for the arrival of Mr Boyle. At last his large body appeared in the doorway. Bella held her breath. She couldn't see both his hands, he was sideways on, but then he turned, and came over to their table, placed both his large, normal hands flat beside the salt pot and leaned over close to Bella's face.

'Had a pleasant day?' he asked, grinning widely as Bella shrank back into her chair.

'Yes, yes, thank you,' she managed to say.

'Mr Bradberry. We haven't seen much of you. Are you very busy? It seems a shame not to enjoy the sun and the sea on your holiday.'

'Thank you, I've had a pleasant day, so far,' said Mr Bradberry.

'Enjoy your meal,' said Mr Boyle and he went off to his own table, nodding a 'good evening' at the other guests as he went.

'No feathers,' said Mr Bradberry.

'No,' Bella agreed sadly, 'but I did get a whiff of fish, I'm sure I did.'

'Not proof, Bella, not proof.'

Chapter Eleven

The following day, Arabella, Billy and Mr Bradberry went down to the sandy beach in the cove below Weatherstone Hall.

The flight of steps, carved into the cliff side, was so narrow that only one person could go up or down at a time.

'Hold on to the rope, Bella,' Mr Bradberry urged as they made their way down. 'It's terribly steep.'

At last they were standing on the sand at the bottom.

'Phew!' said Mr Bradberry. 'I think you should build a lift. Billy, I'm dreading going back up again.'

'Oh, it's not so bad,' said Billy. 'Look, even the Miss Silvers are coming. If they can manage it, I'm sure we should be able to.'

'You're right. I'm very unfit,' agreed Mr Bradberry. 'Well, I shall just sit here in the sun. Er, what about you two?'

'If it's all right with you,' said Billy, 'I'm going to take Bella out in the boat.'

'Fine, fine,' said Mr Bradberry, already leaning back and closing his eyes. 'Life-jackets?'

'Yes, of course.'

'Good. See you later.'

'Look,' said Bella as they walked over to the

far side of the bay where all the boats were moored or pulled up on to the beach. 'There's Mr Boyle. He's got stuck behind the Miss Silvers. By the time they all get down here it'll be time to go back!'

'Yeah, serves him right. I want to stay as far away from him as possible. I kept thinking about his hand and what it might look like all night. Disgusting.'

'Dad didn't believe me.'

'You didn't tell him!'

' 'Course I did. He needs to know Boyle is after the dogs too.'

'Crikey! I'd never tell my mum anything like that, she'd never believe me. I wouldn't believe myself!'

Billy led Arabella to a small wooden rowing boat which was moored alongside the old jetty. The little boat bobbed up and down as the water splashed and gurgled beneath the wooden posts. Gingerly, Bella stepped into it and struggled into her life-jacket. When Billy was also seated, she turned to wave goodbye to her father.

Mr Boyle was standing talking to him.

Quickly she stared up at the rocky steps – the Miss Silvers were still there!

'Billy! Billy!' she cried. 'Look, Boyle's down

on the beach. He beat the Miss Silvers! Now how could he possibly have done that?'

'Do you think he . . .? He couldn't have?'

'He must have! The only way he could have got down to the beach was by flying. Mr Boyle turned into a bird and flew down.'

'I refuse to believe it. I don't want to believe it. Come on, let's get going before he sees us. He really gives me the creeps.'

Bella had never been out in such a tiny boat before and it felt very unsafe and wobbly to begin with, but she grew braver as Billy got into a rhythm and rowed the boat around the coast.

'It's just across there. Seems a long way when you go round the edge. Remember I showed you where the caves were when we saw Miss Longparish?'

Billy rowed hard and soon he shouted, 'There!' and pointed up at the rocky cliffs where darker patches showed like dead black eyes or toothless mouths.

'People say some of them lead into great long tunnels,' he said, 'and they go deep into the cliff. You can't get up to them unless you're a rock-climber or something, otherwise we could investigate.'

'Why are they there?'

'Who knows? Geological faults? Some say old mines, some say smugglers used them.'

Billy stopped rowing and they sat still, letting the boat go free, dipping and rising on the waves. Without the splash of the oars it was suddenly quiet. Seagulls swirled above them and cried so piteously that Arabella shivered.

Billy picked up the oars and rowed the boat close in beneath the caves. The steep overhanging cliffs cast a deep, cold shadow over the water; goosebumps erupted all over Arabella's skin. The noise of the water crashing against the rocks beat all around them like a distant, menacing thunder. The sea below was inky black and choppy and suddenly, the thought of that great depth of water below her made Arabella feel sick and afraid.

'Let's go back,' she said hoarsely.

'You all right?'

'I just don't like it here. And . . . Oh! Billy, look! Look at that enormous fish!'

Billy gasped. 'Crikey!' he cried, peering down at it. 'It's gigantic. Hey! Where's it gone?'

'There it is!'

The little boat tilted dangerously as they leaned over the sides first to the right and then the left, as the great fish darted around them.

It was very big, at least the length of the boat, speckled and spotty with a shimmering purple sheen on its sides that was silver as it angled and lunged below them.

'It's amazing!' cried Billy, leaning right over the side, letting the oars go free. 'I've never seen anything like it. What do you . . . Agh!'

The fantastic fish made a sudden leap straight out of the water, directly into their downturned faces.

The children crashed backwards into the bottom of the boat as the great goggle-eyed fish streaked high into the air, showering them with icy drops of water.

It twirled high above their heads like a performing dolphin, twisting right over the boat and crashing down into the waves on the other side with an almighty splash.

'Have you ever? My goodness!' Billy lunged across the boat to stare down into the water where it had disappeared.

'Watch out!' cried Arabella. She flung herself on to the oars. 'Billy! The rocks! We're going to crash!'

Quick as lightning, Billy grabbed the oars and threw himself back into his seat. He hauled at the oars, pulling for all he was worth, urging the boat away from the deadly jagged rocks and crashing waves.

Arabella crouched, watching the soaring waves and cliffs creep closer. Around them, the water gurgled and spluttered with a choking noise as if it were going down an enormous plug hole and wanted to drag the little boat down with it.

'I can do it! Sit tight! We're pulling away!'

Slowly, the rowing boat shifted out of the

dangerous rocky corner and headed out towards the calmer, bluer sea. As soon as the sun touched their heads again and the heat of its rays warmed them, Arabella felt able to breathe once more.

'Oh, Billy, Billy, that was terrible! I thought we were going to die!'

'Silly. Of course we weren't. Still, it was close. Exciting stuff, hey?' He was grinning merrily.

Arabella didn't reply.

'What a fish! Amazing! I must try and find out what type it was. Never seen one like that before. So big too. It was only because it jumped out like that that we got so close to the cliffs. Odd.'

'Not odd, Billy, not odd at all.'

'What do you mean? Gosh, you're ever so pale, Bella.'

'You can be very dim, Billy,' said Bella, in a small voice.

'I know, but even so . . .'

'You've never seen a fish like that before because you've never had Mr Boyle on holiday here before. Billy, I think that disgusting, ugly-faced fish *was* Mr Boyle!'

Chapter Twelve

Bella found her father sitting in his bedroom amidst a heap of papers and clothes. The mattress had been pulled off the bed and its covers were thrown all over the place. Pictures had even been taken down from the walls.

'Goodness!' cried Bella. 'What has been going on?'

'Good question. I've just come in and found it like this.'

'Someone has been looking for your notes!'

'Yes. You were right. Though not Boyle. Surely he wouldn't have had time. He was on the beach with me earlier.'

If he can fly about like we think he can, thought Bella, he would certainly have had time for everything, including turning into a fish, but she didn't say this to her father.

'So it might have been the great artist,

"Darren Degas", or Miss Longparish, then?'

'I suppose so. I don't like to think about it.'

'And are your notes still there?'

'Yes. No. Well, some of them are.'

'Don't forget we put some in my secret drawer.'

'Of course!' Mr Bradberry suddenly cheered up and smiled. 'I'd completely forgotten that! My newest ideas and theories. What's missing are the notes and diagrams I'd drawn up supposing you could substitute another dog for the eleventh one that's missing. It was just an idea I'd got from some old drawings of Mrs Gumm's. Found them in the library – it's full of the most wonderful old documents. I must persuade her to put them safely in the museum.' He gazed round at the chaos. 'Oh, well, I'll be more careful in future. Bella, not a word to Mrs Gumm! If she thinks there's a problem she might call in somebody else. She might send all the dogs off to a museum. I can't lose her trust now.'

'And are you any closer to finding out where the missing dog is?' asked Bella.

'Of course I am. 'Course I am. Not very close, but definitely closer. Now, what about you? Had a good morning?'

The picture of the horrible wide-mouthed fish swam into Bella's brain with frightening clarity. She saw again its goggle-eyes so like Mr Boyle's . . . Mr Bradberry just wouldn't believe it.

'Fine. Lovely. Very nice. No, nothing exciting,' she said. 'Let's get tidied up, shall we?'

It would only worry him, she thought. Perhaps I'll tell him about it later . . . Much later.

Arabella woke in the night.

She lay for what seemed ages, staring at the gloomy ancient tapestry curtains drawn tightly round her, and thought about the stone dogs and Merlin and the awful Mr Boyle. The embroidered dogs in the tapestry seemed to run round and round and colours became brilliant and vibrant until her tired brain couldn't bear it any longer. She sat up and got out of bed to go to the bathroom.

Outside, grey clouds skudded across a grey sky and the black sea surged and fell on the beach with a soft, shuffling sound.

Over towards the orchard an eerie yellow glow lit the sky. Bella squinted at her watch: 3.30a.m. Was it the sunrise? But no, the light was coming from the ground. It wasn't a fire, there were no flickering shadows or smoke. So what was it?

She pulled on some clothes and crept along the corridor to the staircase which led up to Billy's room. She was just about to place her foot on the first step when she heard a creak from above.

Arabella froze. The hairs on the back of her neck rose; ice ran through her veins. There was another creak, a shuffle . . . someone, or something, was coming down the staircase towards her.

Stepping back quickly, she hid behind the corner and crouched listening and watching.

'BILLY!'

'Aaghh! Bella!' His torch flew up in the air, the floor seemed to slip from under him, and Billy landed on his bottom with a thud.

Arabella helped him up.

'Crikey!' Billy whispered loudly. 'What d'you want to do that for?' He stood up and retrieved his torch. 'You scared me!'

'Sorry. You scared me first.'

'Not as much as you scared me the second time.'

'Sorry. What are you doing?'

'What do you think?'

'Oh, well, so was I until . . . Look out there.' Bella pointed to the light. 'It must be over where the dogs are.'

'I wonder what's going on. Shall we go and see? Dare you?'

' 'Course I dare!'

It was very cold in the garden and a heavy dew made the grass very wet and slippery. Shivering from cold and excitement, they made their way cautiously towards the end of the orchard.

The light came from four storm lanterns which had been placed on the grass amongst the stone dogs. The wedges of yellow light lit up the statues, making them look beautiful and magical; their stony bodies appeared soft, as if they really were furry, and their stone eyes seemed to glint with life.

For several moments the dogs were all Bella saw, then a tall broad figure stepped forward from the shadows and entered the magical circle.

It was Mr Boyle.

Or was it?

The figure had a man's body and legs, but his arms were not arms, but wings which he held wide open, spreading his magnificent feathers. But it was his head which was the worst. Bella trembled, looking at it, unable to tear her eyes from it.

The head of the man was that of a fish. The fish that had almost overturned their boat.

'Oh, no. Horrible. I don't like it. I want to go,' whispered Bella, but she was frozen to the spot, just like Billy, and all they could do was crouch by the wall and stare.

'It's not working, gov'nor.' McGregor stepped into the circle of light. There was a hint of satisfaction in his voice. He tapped the nearest stone dog on the head. 'Hard as rocks.'

'Shut up!' The fish-man's voice was nasty, flat and cold.

Arabella squeezed Billy's arm.

'Look,' she said. 'There's a real dog there, beside the stone ones. Black and white.'

'So there is. What do . . .?'

'I know, I know, they're trying to break the spell using a real dog. My father told me. It was an idea he had. Oh, I hope it won't work. Don't let it work.'

Mr Boyle pulled himself up as tall as possible, threw back his arms and swept open his wonderful wings.

'Weatherstone. Weatherstone. Weatherstone.' His voice rumbled deeply like a train coming up through a tunnel. 'Come on, my beauties!'

'What now? What shall I do with this dog?' asked McGregor, who had the little dog on a lead. It was shivering with fright.

'I don't know, do I?' Mr Boyle looked round crossly. 'Drat these wings!' he added. 'They get in the way. Bradberry's notes said something about their names and joining them in a circle, but he was only guessing.'

Mr Boyle suddenly let out a shriek and snatched at his arms.

'What is it, boss? What's the matter?' McGregor ran to his side and grabbed him, and it seemed that as he touched him the feathers disappeared and the man's normal arms appeared.

Boyle flexed his arms and fingers again and smiled.

'That's better. I have to think so hard to control it. I have to fight it. It keeps trying to creep up on me.'

'OK, boss, OK, but what shall we do with these dogs?'

'Link them with this rope, tie it round their necks.' McGregor did as he was told. 'Now I'll stand in the centre and call their names out . . . except we don't know the name of the eleventh . . . and say Bradberry's rhyme. Come on, hurry up.'

'It won't work,' Bella whispered to Billy. 'Not like that, I just know it won't.'

When the rope circle was complete, Boyle stood in the middle and began his magic, calling out the dogs' names, trying to break the spell.

'Come again, break from the past,
Throw off your gritty, stony cast.
Ye eleven magical dogs of old
As once for Merlin, now find BOYLE *GOLD*!'

It was eerie watching his bulbous fish-lips move and human words come out of them. His skin glistened purple and pink and blue in the lantern light and the scales on his cheeks and neck shone silver.

The children stared at him and at the stone dogs.

McGregor shifted uneasily.

'Nothing, boss. Dead as dodos.'

Boyle shouted angrily, kicking out at the statues.

'Change, Why don't you! Change!' he roared, but the stone dogs didn't move.

'Let's get back to the house,' McGregor suggested with a shiver. 'I'll let this little fellow find his own way back to the village, shall I?'

He released the black and white dog which scampered happily off home.

'All right, all right,' sighed Boyle. 'We'll give up for now.'

'Come on, Billy,' urged Bella. 'We'd better hurry. We don't want them to see us out here!'

They turned and hurried back through the garden.

It was light now. A pale sun was showing across the bay and the sky was white, no longer grey.

Somehow, perhaps because Bella was leading the way, they didn't go back to the house on the normal route but branched off along a new path, over towards the other side of the garden where the greenhouses were.

Here the branches hung so low that they had to bend double to pass. Creeping leaves and scratching thorns fought against their entry, but still Bella forged on.

'We've come the wrong way,' said Billy. 'What are you doing? Ouch! Let's turn round.'

Suddenly, Bella found she could stand. They had come to a little clearing where the leaves above almost joined overhead, forming an emerald arching roof like a tiny theatre. They were in a small, circular place, completely hidden and secret from the rest of the garden.

Directly in front of them, staring straight at them, it seemed, was the most wonderful statue of a dog.

'Oh, Billy, look!' she breathed. 'Isn't it lovely!'

The dog wasn't stone; it was made of hundreds and hundreds of broken pieces of pottery,

stuck together in a patchwork of mosaic. Colours leapt from its surface, orange spots on one fragment, brilliant turquoise on another, gold filigree over there. The dog's eyes, shimmering as though the sea were trapped inside them, seemed to look right into theirs. It was quite the most beautiful dog that Bella had ever seen.

'Well!' said Billy. 'How peculiar. I never knew this was here. And look,' he added. 'All around it the garden's been done. There are no weeds, just flowers, and the path is cleared and everything.'

'Who could have done it?'

'It *must* be Uncle Jack. It must be. He's the only gardener. But why? I recognize the pottery, you know. Do you?' Bella shook her head. 'It's bits of our stuff from the house. There are bits of all our oddments here.'

'How very strange. Very odd.'

'But wonderful! And surely, Bella – I can't think why you haven't thought of this – surely this must be the missing dog! This is number eleven!'

'Well . . .'

'It must be!' cried Billy. 'Oh, I can't wait to see your father's face. He'll be so thrilled!' He looked nervously over his shoulder, suddenly remembering Boyle and McGregor. 'We must be careful. We mustn't let those others find it.'

'I'm not sure this is the eleventh dog, Billy,' said Bella. 'I don't know why, but I don't recognize it like I did the others and it doesn't look quite the same. But . . .'

'You're just jealous 'cos you didn't think of it first,' said Billy smugly. 'Come on. Let's go home!'

Chapter Thirteen

When Bella got back to her bedroom she was so exhausted she fell into bed fully clothed and slept immediately.

It was late when she woke and a note propped up beside her bed said: 'Gone to the village. See you later. Love Dad.'

So Bella went down for breakfast on her own. Billy was the only other person in the dining-room.

'I'm in trouble with Mum for sleeping in this morning and not helping,' he said. 'I've got to change all the tablecloths. Huh!'

'I'll help.'

Billy thanked her. 'Wasn't that amazing last night? Phew! That Boyle is a monster! Have you told your dad what he was up to last night? And about the mosaic dog we found?'

'Shh!' Bella warned, looking round anxiously. 'You never know who might be listening.'

'Oh, yeah, Bella,' Billy agreed, grinning widely. 'Watch out for the giant slugs in the windowbox – they can read your mind!'

'Very funny. No, honestly, Billy, I really thought I saw someone flit past the window.'

Suddenly Lady began barking. She had been sitting quietly at Bella's feet and now she jumped up and barked furiously.

'What is it? What's the matter?'

Billy flew to the window and was just in time to see Darren McGregor's back as he disappeared into the bushes.

'I take it all back,' said Billy, glumly. 'McGregor *was* out there. He couldn't have heard us, could he? He wouldn't know what I meant, anyway.'

'I hope not. We didn't say much. Oh, nowhere's safe around here. We must be careful!'

'Well, the great artist's gone now. Come on, I'm dying to tell your dad about the "you-know-what" dog!'

'He's not here. He's gone out to the village for something. Perhaps he's got a clue? Actually, Billy, I was just wondering about his notes . . .'

'What about them?'

'Well, what's he found out? He said he'd got some new clues. I just thought we might take a look.'

'Isn't that sort of stealing?'

'We're not going to take them away. No, it's sort of borrowing. They're in my desk. I'm sure he'd tell us if he were here to ask. I don't want to waste any time. I feel as if it's all such a race. Come on, let's do these tablecloths and hurry up.'

When the tables were done, they went upstairs to Bella's bedroom where Bella showed Billy the secret drawer.

'Pooh, I knew it was there all the time,' said Billy, who hadn't. 'I'm surprised Boyle or McGregor didn't find it when they stole your dad's notes.'

'Too simple for the adult brain,' said Bella.

She opened the drawer and took out her father's notes which were written on postcard-size bits of paper.

There were sheets and sheets covered with Mr Bradberry's cramped, tiny writing: maps with strange signs and characters, plans over-laced with intricate diagrams and ciphers, charts with numbers and Arabic-looking designs, and

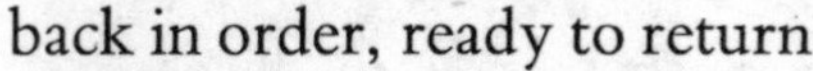

lists and lists of figures and strange words.

'Crikey!' said Billy. 'Impossible!'

'Oh, what a shame,' said Bella, disappointed. 'I really thought we might get some clues.' She shuffled the notes back in order, ready to return to the drawer. 'I suppose Dad knows what he's doing, but . . . there's something wrong here. There's too much science and not enough . . .'

'Enough what?'

'Enough *understanding*. He can't see the wood for the trees.'

'Too deep for me. Come on, put them back.'

Bella was just doing so, when she saw something at the back of the drawer.

'Oh, look, there's a bit more paper in there.'

She stretched her arm inside and, right up against the back, her fingers touched another small sheet of paper wedged in the woodwork. She pulled it out.

'This isn't his,' she said. 'Look, different paper and different writing. It's a letter.'

'Let's have a look.'

The letter was dated 4 June. The address at the top was Weatherstone Hall. The paper was purple and so was the faded ink it was written in. It seemed to be very faintly scented. A dim rosy-garden smell seemed to drift around them as they read.

My Darling Jack,
By the time you read this I will have gone out of your life for ever.
We can never be together while your mother is so against me and she always will be; she always has been.
I'm sorry I wasn't born in a big house like you, sorry that I'm so clumsy and silly. If you marry me against her wishes she'll cut you off without a penny — I don't care for myself but you'd hate it, my love.
Darling, I shall never forget you, never, never, <u>never</u>. When you go back to our secret meeting place and see what's there I hope you'll smile & remember me and always remember me.
Yours forever & ever,
Clementine
♡

PS I shall be at Windrush Farm until Tuesday if you want me.

'How romantic!' Arabella cried. 'It's from Uncle Jack's fiancée. She didn't leave him without a word, like he thought . . . What secret place in the garden? What monument? And why didn't he get this letter?'

'This desk belonged to his mother, my great-grandmother. He's my great-uncle, really. Do you think she kept it from him? Mother says she was an old trout, always bossing the family about.'

'If she did, it was very wicked of her. It says: "Cut you off without a penny." Was there money then?'

'Yes,' Billy said. 'A long time ago. It's all gone now.'

'It must have been wonderful in the old days . . . You would have more money if you had more guests. There's lots of space; hundreds of empty rooms . . .'

'Have you looked in any of those empty rooms?'

'No, why?'

'They don't have ceilings.'

'Oh.'

'Or floors.'

'Oh, well, I didn't . . .'

'And some of them don't even have walls.'

'I see. Well, if we find the eleventh dog and then find Merlin's grave, this place will be so famous you'll be swamped with visitors . . . and nowhere to put them . . . A campsite?'

'Silly. It's very difficult. First we need lots and lots of money to put things straight, then we could have one or two more guests to make it pay. But then it won't be like this. And I do love it.' He gazed up at the cracked ceiling and smiled. 'Don't you?'

Bella nodded. Just then they heard Mrs Gumm calling Billy.

'Oh no, not again! It's Mum. What does she want now?'

They hurried out of the room and bumped straight into Miss Longparish.

'Sorry!' Billy yelled, dashing off and leaving Bella to make amends.

Miss Longparish and Bella bounced apart like spongy toys and fell to the floor. The books and fishing tackle Miss Longparish had been carrying flew up in the air and the large fishing basket upturned, sending a plump dead fish slithering out on to the floorboards.

The smell was terrible!

'Pooh!' cried Bella. 'Oh, gosh, what a stink . . . I mean, sorry, Miss Longparish.'

'Oh dear, oh dear,' said the woman, struggling to her knees and beginning to gather up her things. 'My fish, I think.' She thrust it into the basket again, but the dreadful smell lingered on. 'Bass,' she explained. 'Freshly caught. Delicious.'

It was such an enormous lie, such an obvious lie, that for a few seconds they stared at each other in amazement; Arabella wondering how Miss Longparish dared lie so terribly, and Miss Longparish no doubt wondering the same thing.

The moment passed and they gathered up the rest of the fishing things from along the corridor.

'I'm really very sorry,' Bella said again. 'We weren't looking.'

'Don't worry. Not at all. Thank you. Thank you.'

Bella stacked the books together. A photograph was sticking out of one and Bella caught sight of it and froze.

She got a good long look at it before she slipped it out of sight inside the book.

It was the very same photo that Billy and she had seen in Uncle Jack's den – the one of him and Clementine.

I'd never have thought it possible, Bella thought. She seems so nice, and yet Miss Longparish is not only a liar, but a thief as well!

Chapter Fourteen

When Billy had finished the chores for his mother, he and Bella took the old letter they'd found to show to Uncle Jack.

Lady joined them in the garden and Billy threw her sticks which she chased and brought back to them.

'She's so lovely,' said Bella. 'I do wish I could

have a dog. I've always, always wanted one.'

'I bet your dad will give you a hundred if we find the eleventh stone dog,' said Billy.

'But I only want one,' said Bella. 'One just like Lady.'

They found Uncle Jack shooting arrows at a target on the long lawn at the back of the house. The two Miss Silvers sat nearby in the shade of a large mulberry tree, embroidering handkerchiefs.

'We found this, Uncle Jack. We think it really belongs to you.' She handed him the letter. 'Sorry we read it, but if we hadn't, we wouldn't have known to give it to you.'

She took a few steps back, leaving him to read it in peace.

Uncle Jack read it once, then very slowly, mouthing the words, read it again. Bella watched his face. It was pale and rigidly composed and yet she knew he must be seething with emotions, like one of her mother's heroines in her books.

At last, Uncle Jack folded the letter up and tucked it neatly inside his trouser pocket. Still he didn't speak. He picked up his bow and arrow again, then, very slowly, aimed it and shot.

The 'twang' sounded loud and hard, but it

wasn't a good shot and the arrow missed the target entirely, very nearly skewering one Miss Silver to the bench.

'Sorry, Uncle Jack,' said Billy. 'We found it in grandmother's old desk and knew it must be for you. Grandmother must have hidden it.'

'She must, the mean old trout. The sort of thing she would do. Oh, if only someone had found it sooner! So many years have passed! I thought she didn't love me. We had a secret meeting-place – I waited, went every day – nothing, nothing except the statue . . . Oh, Clementine! It's my own fault, of course,' he burbled on. 'I was too proud. I was looking for Merlin's grave then, too. To have my own money and my own fame. Oh, foolish youth! She was clumsy though, oh, my goodness . . .' and he chuckled. 'Time. Youth . . . I wasted it all away.'

The children looked at each other. Billy shrugged.

Uncle Jack started whistling softly: 'Oh my darling, oh my darling Clementine,' and, without another word, walked off.

'How romantic,' said Bella. 'Perhaps I could write a book about it. It's just the sort of thing my mother writes about.'

'It's twaddle,' said Billy, 'so don't waste your time.'

Mr Bradberry arrived back at Weatherstone Hall just in time for lunch.

'Where have you been, Dad? I've been desperate to see you.' She glanced round nervously. They were standing in the great hall and it was full of dark corners and cupboards that could house spies.

'You'll never guess what happened to us last night! Billy and I saw Boyle and McGregor out in the garden trying to get the dogs alive.'

'My goodness!'

'Yes, and it *must* have been them who stole your notes because they were trying the magic with another dog – one from the village – and you said that was your idea.'

'But it didn't work?'

'No, it didn't.'

'Good, I didn't think it would. Well, Bella, so you were right about them, eh? I wonder who Boyle really is? I'm sure I've seen him before, I recognize that pony tail and those haddock eyes, but I just can't place him. Perhaps we've met at a conference or on a "dig". He must know something about archaeology . . .'

'And he knew your rhyme.'

'What!'

'Yes, he did, because he said it.'

'That is bad. Very bad. But how ? How could he possibly? I didn't even write it down anywhere – except at home and at the museum . . . at the museum, perhaps . . . Oh, well, he can't know all the things I know. I'm one step ahead, don't you worry, Bella . . .'

'Yes, but Dad, there's something else . . .'

'Wait, wait, let me tell you what *I* was doing this morning. I've worked out, scientifically, exactly where the eleventh dog is!'

'You have?' Bella sounded doubtful.

'I have. And this afternoon a man with a heavy-duty digging machine is coming up from the village to excavate the spot.'

'Oh, Dad!'

'What?'

'It's just, well, are you sure?'

'Ninety-nine per cent.'

Mr Bradberry seemed so pleased with himself that Bella hadn't the heart to tell him about the mosaic dog. I'll show it to him when he doesn't find anything this afternoon, she thought. Billy will be disappointed too, though, because I don't think the mosaic dog is the eleventh either. They're both wrong, I feel sure they are, but I don't know why!

Mr Bradberry, Mrs Gumm, Lady and the two children gathered in the garden to watch the man with the excavator dig for the stone dogs. Although she hadn't seen McGregor or Boyle, Bella was sure they would be watching from somewhere.

Mr Bradberry was explaining to Mrs Gumm how he'd worked out precisely where the eleventh dog should be.

'You see,' he said, 'it was knowing the dogs had been lifted out in a circle like that. It had to be important. It was just a matter of working out the astronomical and astrological connotations. I worked it all out with mathematics and statistics and ley lines and logarithms. Science can't be wrong.'

Mrs Gumm nodded, bemused but fascinated.

'What's that word that means knowing something without knowing why?' asked Bella. 'I mean, knowing something automatically. Just knowing the answer.'

'Intuition,' said Mrs Gumm.

'That's it,' said Bella. 'That's what you've forgotten, Dad, I knew there was something.'

Mr Bradberry smiled and was about to reply when Syd, the man on the digging machine, called out he was ready and would they stand back.

The little gathering moved up on to a grassy mound to watch as the yellow machine ploughed noisily towards its allocated place, its tooth-edged shovel poised in the air.

'It's like a prehistoric monster,' said Bella, feeling alarmed.

'Very strong,' said her father.

The shovel drove into the soil and churned up a large furrow of brown earth. It repeated the same movement several times until Mr Bradberry signalled for it to stop.

'It would have taken me a week to dig that out,' said Mr Bradberry. 'Wonderful. Wonderful. Let's just take a look, we don't want to damage anything. Stand back, everyone. I'll go over and see.'

Syd looked round his door, signalled to Mr Bradberry and jumped down from his machine, leaving the motor humming gently. Tipping back his cap, he went over to join Mr Bradberry.

Then it happened. There was no warning, not until Bella let out a loud shriek, but that came too late.

The heavy yellow machine suddenly rumbled into a different gear and began to trundle over the grass towards Mr Bradberry.

Mr Bradberry looked up just in time to see the great machine towering above him. He couldn't hear the shrieks and cries of warning from the others, only the roar and rattle of the engine, loud in his ears as he made a desperate jump for safety.

Within seconds, Syd had leapt into the driver's cab and turned off the digger's engine.

The sudden silence was intense. Bella, Billy and Mrs Gumm rushed to Mr Bradberry's side and gazed down at him.

'Oh, Dad!' cried Bella. 'Dad!'

Like a puppet without its strings, her father lay all twisted and still on the brown, newly turned earth, eyes closed and deathly pale.

Chapter Fifteen

In the early evening, Mrs Gumm telephoned the hospital where Mr Bradberry had been rushed by ambulance after the accident.

Bella watched Mrs Gumm's face intently, anxious for any clue about her father.

Mrs Gumm was smiling. Did that mean he was all right?

'How is he? What's the news?' Bella blurted out as soon as Mrs Gumm had put down the phone.

'Fine. The nurse said he's fine, so you can stop worrying. It looked much worse than it was. A broken leg, a twisted ankle and a sprained shoulder. It sounds a lot, but honestly, my dear, I thought it was going to be worse too.'

'Oh, thank goodness! Can I go and see him now?'

'No, they said he was going to rest. Don't look so worried! He's got to have his leg put in plaster and get some sleep, then he'll be back tomorrow. That's not long to wait, is it? And he doesn't want your mother informed – said she'd only fret. He had a message for you, apparently. He said to send you his love and that he misses you and also, I think this was right, to watch out for Dylan Hockney . . . Does that mean anything to you?'

Bella nodded.

'Yes,' she said. 'It's a sort of joke.' She looked across at Billy, sitting beside Lady, and stroking her soft head. 'Isn't it, Billy?'

Billy nodded.

'Right. Good. Now, you two go off and play and try and forget all about this nasty accident. Poor Syd has had to take the rest of the day off, too, it was such a shock. He swears he put the brake on. Says he's never had an accident before in his life. Can't understand it. Now, off you go and cheer up, Bella. Your father is absolutely . . . well, almost fine.'

It was good to get away from the house and out into the fresh air. The children wandered out to the edge of the cliff and sat on the rocks overlooking the sea. It was sunny again, and only the merest breeze rippled the water and ruffled their hair.

'Mmm, it's lovely out here,' said Bella, breathing in the sea smells of salt and sand and wild flowers. 'I feel as if I've been here for ages, or been here before, or know it somehow. I feel really at home.'

'I think lots of visitors do. It's what makes them come back year after year, like the Miss Silvers.'

'Yes. I think I can cross them off my list of suspects, but I shall keep Miss Longparish on still. She's definitely up to something . . .'

They were both avoiding talking about what worried them most. There was a long silence while they stared out at the sea, watching a little boat cross the bay and holiday-makers down on the beach.

'You know that message from your father . . .' said Billy.

'Yes, yes, I know.'

'He meant McGregor, didn't he? He knew, didn't he?'

'I suppose he must have. Did you see him?'

'I only saw him afterwards, running away, and then I realized it must have been him that took the brake off, but it was too late.'

'Me too. I don't know how he crept up there without us seeing him,' agreed Bella. 'The sneaking little weasel! What a horrid thing to do! He could have killed Dad, really killed him.'

'I know. It means we have to be very, very careful, Bella,' said Billy, glancing around quickly. 'Nowhere's safe. Nobody's to be trusted.'

'They must know everything we know, that's what I hate,' said Bella. 'I keep looking over my shoulder and wanting to whisper.'

'Do you think they know about the mosaic dog?'

'I don't know. Did McGregor hear us the other morning? Have they already taken it away to join the circle of stone dogs?'

'Let's go and see. Come on. Anything's better than just doing nothing,' said Billy.

They walked back along the clifftops to the house and into the walled garden through a side gate.

'Can you remember where it was?'

'It's your garden, Billy, you should know.'

'But it was you who took us there that night.'

'Yes, but I did it by mistake. I was on automatic pilot.'

'Well, it was over by the greenhouses, I

remember that. And we were coming up from the field where the dogs are, so we'll have to try and retrace our steps.'

Eventually, the children found themselves back on the tiny path again, but it seemed not as overgrown as before and less tidy, as if a large animal had pushed its way roughly through the branches and flowers, crushing them and pulling them out of its way.

Neither Billy nor Bella spoke, but their fears grew as they approached the secret bower, their senses telling them something was wrong.

Everything was ruined.

The flowers were trampled on, the leaves stripped from the trees, and the poor little statue – it was smashed to pieces.

Bella let out a cry and fell to her knees beside the splintered fragments of the mosaic dog which littered the earth. She wept as she gathered them up in her hands, filling her arms with the pieces.

'Oh, how mean, how mean,' she kept on repeating. 'The rotten stinkers. The rats! The creeps!'

'They beat us to it again!' said Billy. 'But why do this, if it was the eleventh of Merlin's dogs?' He knelt down beside Bella, close, but too shy

to touch her. 'It must have been Boyle and McGregor who smashed it up, but why?

'Because it *wasn't* the eleventh dog,' sobbed Bella. 'It never was, I told you it wasn't. It was something else, something special . . .'

'You are quite right, my dear, it was something very special,' said a voice behind them.

The children spun round in amazement.

It was Miss Longparish.

Chapter Sixteen

Miss Longparish stepped in beside them and sank on to a small stone seat almost hidden beneath ivy and honeysuckle. She removed the thick veil from her head and draped it round her shoulders. She smiled kindly at the children, but her eyes were sad.

'It was my dog,' she said at last. 'I made it.'

'You did?' Billy was amazed.

'Yes. I was a maid here once, a long time ago when your great-grandmother was alive, Billy, and the family was rich. Jack and I fell in love but that mean old trout – I beg her pardon, his mother – wouldn't have any of it. She thought I wasn't good enough! Pah!'

'People don't bother with things like that nowadays,' said Bella. 'Do they?'

'I would hope not. And, of course, I should

have been stronger and so should Jack. We could have eloped – anything. But Jack had this idea he could find Merlin's grave . . . you know all the stories about him being buried around here? He spent all his energies looking for it. Waste of time, waste of time. And I was so clumsy, broke things all the time. Cups, plates, dishes . . . Mrs Gumm shouted and called me names but she wouldn't sack me, oh no, she knew she'd never get another maid like me to put up with her bossing and bullying . . .' She sighed and fell silent.

'Go on, Miss Longparish, go on,' Bella urged.

'Well, I kept all those bits of broken china, though I don't know why. Then Jack and I had a really big row and I was so upset and broke a soup tureen – old Delftware it was, worth a fortune – and Mrs Gumm nearly had a fit!' She smiled. 'It's not funny, really. Anyway, then I made this little dog. It was a replica of the dog the family had at the time – Princess she was called, lovely animal, lovely. Though I'm still not sure why I did it.'

'Perhaps it was therapeutic,' said Bella, helpfully. 'Like sick people do in hospital.'

'Maybe it was.'

'You must have broken an awful lot of pots!' said Billy, thinking of all the odd pieces of china left at home.

'Hundreds,' said Miss Longparish with some pride.

'Miss Longparish,' Arabella said softly, 'is Longparish really your name?'

'No, dear, it isn't.'

'And you're not an angler, are you?'

'Oh dear, you guessed then? I thought you might have. You see, I thought I'd come back here and give it one final chance. I thought Jack might just still love me but I wanted to be sure . . .'

'And he does! He does!' cried Bella. 'Doesn't he, Billy?'

'Does he?' asked Billy. He hadn't yet worked out who Miss Longparish really was.

'I believe you're right,' said Miss Longparish, smiling gently. 'I've watched him carefully and I've heard him playing that record and seen how he tended this little patch of garden so beautifully. But then why didn't he ever write? Why didn't he follow me to Windrush Farm?'

'Do you mean your name is . . .' Billy began, the truth dawning at last. He grinned. 'Golly . . .'

But before he could finish, they were interrupted by the noise of someone else approaching and, looking up, they saw Uncle Jack pushing his way through the bushes.

He paused for a moment on the edge of the bower, standing rock-like, his face pale and eyes bright, then he lurched forward, arms outstretched, calling, 'CLEMENTINE! Clementine, my darling, darling girl!'

Jack clung to her like ivy clings to a stone wall, and their whispering and kisses bubbled up from them and overflowed beneath the leafy roof and seemed to fill the little bower until there was no room for Billy and Arabella. Quickly and quietly they tiptoed away.

'Phew!' exclaimed Billy when they were out in the open again. 'Aren't they a bit old for all that? Hope Uncle Jack doesn't give himself a heart attack or something.'

'Silly! It'll do him good. I bet you anything they get married now and he'll start gardening again. I'm so glad she turned out nice and not a baddie like Boyle and McGregor.'

'Yes . . . they couldn't have found anything in the hole that was excavated then, or they wouldn't have done this,' Billy said. 'So they needn't have done that to your father after all! They should have waited and watched. Did they overhear us talk about the mosaic dog, do you think? They must have smashed it when they realized that it wasn't the dog they wanted either. Vandals! Louts!'

'Better than smashing us up, Billy, like they did my dad,' said Bella. 'I think they're getting more and more desperate. If Boyle's magic power is going wonky, then they'll want to find that eleventh dog as soon as possible, before he has none at all!'

Chapter Seventeen

The following morning, Mr Bradberry returned to Weatherstone Hall. He looked pale and was in some pain, but seemed very cheerful.

'Don't look so worried, Bella dear,' he told her. 'And don't even think about contacting your mother, do you hear me? I couldn't do with her fussing around here too!'

'But you can't walk or anything. How will you manage?'

'I can hobble with these crutches, and Mrs Gumm – wonderful woman – says I can have a bed downstairs. I shall continue my research in the library and you will have to do any running about for me.'

'Well, of course I will,' said Bella. 'Anything you want.'

'Good. Now, the other thing I want – and

this is most important – is for you to take care.' He lowered his voice. 'Big machines like that do not start going on their own, you know.'

'I do know.'

'Was I right to think it was McGregor?'

'Billy and I saw him running away, just after the digger moved,' said Bella. 'But Boyle will have ordered him to do it. He's the boss.'

'Hmm.' Bradberry looked thoughtful.

'It's Boyle that's the really dangerous one, Dad. I wish you'd believe me. He can change shape, he honestly can.'

Her father ignored her.

'I hear a statue has got broken. A statue of a dog.'

'Yes, but it wasn't the eleventh stone dog, it was made of pottery pieces and Miss Longparish made it and she's really Clementine, Uncle Jack's long-lost love.'

'Really?' Mr Bradberry raised his eyebrows in amazement. 'I am glad your mother's not here, she'd be taking notes for her next novel.'

After lunch Mr Bradberry limped back to the library to continue his research. Bella mooched around, wondering what to do. Billy was doing chores for his mother and it was no fun outside as a fine, cool drizzle was falling.

She lingered beside the fire in the great hall, gazing up at the enormous tapestries that covered the bare stone walls. They were beautifully done and very old; some had threadbare patches and were faded, but she could just make out the pictures, which showed castles, gardens, forests and oddly dressed people of long ago. One she found especially interesting, and she was just about to climb the stairs to examine it more closely, when she heard her father calling excitedly.

'Bella! Bella! Come here, Bella!'

He sounded so excited that Billy came running too and together they burst into the library, expecting to find Mr Boyle there or the place on fire, but there was only Mr Bradberry, lying on the couch, waving some papers at them.

'Come in! Come in! I just have to share this with someone.' Then, in a lower voice: 'Bella, check there's nobody in the hall . . . Billy, check outside the window. We must be careful!'

The children did as they were asked. The hall was clear; Bella closed and locked the big oak door firmly. Billy peered out of the windows; no-one was lurking beneath the sill or crouching in the nearby bushes.

But there was something Billy did not see.

Growing up alongside the library window was an old wisteria plant whose stems were gnarled and twisted with age. Wrapped around that stem, looped and bent like a bit of vegetation, was a long, slender green snake with bizarre goggly eyes . . .

'It's all clear,' said Billy, joining Mr Bradberry and Bella. 'Nothing.'

'Good. Come and see this,' said Mr Bradberry, indicating the papers on the low table beside his couch. 'It's fascinating. It's a journal written by one Archibald Winterstoke Gumm in seventeen seventy-two. He's describing the alterations they're having done on the house. Apparently there was a fountain in the courtyard . . .'

'That's right!' said Bella.

'. . . don't interrupt . . . and when they dismantled it, they found an old inscription. Listen:

> It was with great sadness that my men began the break-up and removal of the ancient marble fountain which has for so many years graced the eastern courtyard. My gentle Phoebe could not but shed tears on so sad an occasion. The great shell dish which was so badly cracked was the last piece to be removed and it was found to be resting on a stone plinth on which ancient letters were engraved. Sir Edward and I fell on this with great enthusiasm, we both being such keen historians. Our interest and delight was enormous when we found, yet again, another reference to what can only be Merlin's magical pack of dogs, so firing our

determination to discover their whereabouts
at whatever cost to body or soul . . .'

'But what did it say? What was carved on the stone?' cried Billy.

'The Honourable Mr Gumm has very thoughtfully copied the inscription down for us. Ready?'

The children nodded.

'Gold-hunters, ten in number,
Granite cold they rest and slumber.
For revival, complete the pack.
With maiden thou shalt bring them back.'

'Does it make any sense to you?' asked Billy. 'I'm afraid I don't understand. Why are there only ten in that rhyme and what do they mean about the maiden?'

Mr Bradberry smiled. 'It's not very clear, is it. But, of course, if it means what I think it means, it doesn't help us anyway . . .'

'Why not?'

'Because I'd never do it.'

'Do what?' asked Billy, more puzzled than ever.

Mr Bradberry looked at Bella.

'Well, daughter of mine, have you any idea?'

'Yes,' said Bella. She looked at her father with shining eyes and flushed cheeks. 'Yes, Dad. It means *I* could take the place of the missing dog, complete the pack and break the spell!'

Silence.

Billy stared at her in astonishment.

Mr Bradberry shook his head.

'No, Bella. I wouldn't dream of it.'

'But that's what it says! A maiden, like me. Of course it would be, wouldn't it, because the dogs are all female too. Oh, Dad, let me try. If we could get them back to life they'd lead you to Merlin's grave, you'd get your professorship, and Billy would get rich from all the tourists. Come on, Dad, say yes, say yes!'

'Bella, Bella, just think for a moment,' said her father, gently. 'What do you suppose would happen, just supposing the rhyme was actually true, of course. How would it work? What would happen to you? If you took the place of the missing dog, Bella, just think! You might never come back! You might get turned to stone and never come back!'

Chapter Eighteen

'I should never have told you,' said Mr Bradberry, closing the diary and shuffling his papers together. 'I wish I'd never seen old what's-his-name's notes.'

'Oh, don't say that, Dad,' Bella begged. 'It's wonderful that you found it. It probably wouldn't work anyway. I mean, who put that inscription on the stone in the first place? And why? Did anyone try it, do you think? He might have made it all up just for fun, just for someone to find years and years later, like you have.'

'I don't think so, somehow,' said Mr Bradberry. 'For the first time, I feel it's right. You do, too, don't you?'

Bella had to agree.

'But one can't go around sacrificing young girls for the advancement of one's own career,' said Mr Bradberry. 'I shall just have to find another way. There *must* be another way. Look at all these journals and documents, letters and maps! They all relate to the Weatherstone estate. I shall go on looking. Yes, I shan't be defeated. It might have worked – but no, probably not. I shall disregard the information. Quite.'

'Sorry, Dad.'

'Don't apologize. Not your fault, Bella. But you do understand, don't you? I couldn't risk it, I couldn't try and use my own daughter to bring the dogs back to life, I just couldn't.'

'I agree, Mr Bradberry,' said Billy. 'It wouldn't be honourable.'

'Quite,' agreed Mr Bradberry. 'There must be another way, there must, and I shall find it!'

The children went out into the hall.

'Poor Dad,' Bella said. 'He's so disappointed.' She sank into the enormous armchair beside the fire and gazed into the flames. Lady rested her delicate chin on Bella's lap, gazing up at her with mournful eyes. 'You know we're upset, don't you, Lady? Good girl. We can't even take you for a walk – it's raining. Oh dear, what shall we do now?'

'I wish your father wasn't so honourable,' said Billy. 'I bet it would have worked and then we'd have been rich.'

'Don't worry about me, will you? I wonder if he'd have let you take the place of the eleventh . . . Oh well, at least the Boyle doesn't know about it.' She looked round, nervously. 'Dad'll have to guard that new rhyme with his life!'

'Absolutely. Crikey, it would be awful if they got hold of it . . . Oh, crumbs, look at the time – better go and help Mum,' said Billy. 'Are you all right on your own?'

'I've got Lady – of course I am. I shall read a book or something. See you later.'

Billy went off down one of the long, dark

corridors which led to the kitchen, and all was quiet again.

Bella found herself once more staring up at the wonderful tapestries hanging on the walls.

I never did get a close look at that one, she reminded herself, and she climbed halfway up the stairs to the landing where a faded cloth hung.

She recognized the large building in the centre of the tapestry as Weatherstone Hall as it must have been when first built. How odd, she thought, that the old castle, with slit windows and ramparts, was once considered modern – the latest thing! Now all that remained of that first house were heaps of broken stones, derelict towers and crumbling walls.

The men in the picture wore tabards and tights and shoes with long, pointy toes. Some carried swords and others had bows and arrows. Women wearing long skirts and strange head-dresses leaned out of the castle windows, sat sewing in the sunlit garden or walked amongst the flowers.

Dogs were embroidered all around the border of the tapestry. Here they were running, here chasing a deer, here gathered around a tall man dressed in faded purple. They were the same long-legged, slender-bodied dogs as the stone statues in the garden. They had the same beautiful, intelligent faces and muscular bodies, but the tapestry dogs were much more alive, with shining eyes and glistening coats. They must be Merlin's dogs, Bella thought, and though they were fabricated in wool and silken stitches, they looked real enough to bark.

As she scrutinized the vast cloth, the strangest sensations began to creep up on Bella. It was as

if the colours were getting brighter and the shapes and figures more defined and more real. Then, as she stared harder and harder, it seemed as though the people began to move and she became dimly aware of muffled, distant noises.

At first she couldn't distinguish separate sounds, it was just a blur, then from out of the hubbub came the distinct rustling of the wind in the trees, the murmur of waves breaking gently on the shore, and the sharp sound of a dog barking. As the figures moved, she even heard the knights' armour clanking and the ladies' dresses swishing.

A young man with a short, dark beard appeared and Bella felt a stab of recognition, almost a pain at seeing this sweet, loving face again. The man came running through the garden towards her, calling: 'Lady Isabelle. Lady Isabelle!' Laughing, Bella leaned forward to reply, but the words died on her lips.

It wasn't to her that he called, she could see that now: the Lady Isabelle was a young girl at the castle window. But as Bella stared at the laughing young face, framed by dark twisting plaits, her disappointment faded because the girl was just like her, like Bella. It was Bella, a Bella of long ago.

'Arthur! Where are you going? Won't you take me walking with you?' called the Lady Isabelle, and Bella, standing on the hall stairs, mouthed the words, knowing what was coming next as if she had spoken them only yesterday.

'No, my pretty little niece. I have a meeting with the wise one. I must go alone. I just came to bring you these.' He flung up a bunch of white roses tied with red ribbon.

'Thank you. They're beautiful. You won't go quite alone, I fancy. Do the dogs go with you?'

'Aye, well, the little one, your namesake, does.' And patting his thigh, he called to one of the golden-haired dogs who was sniffing the grass nearby. 'Farewell, little Lady!' he cried, and man and dog began to walk away from the house, across the open grassland towards the sea.

Bella wanted to see the girl at the window again, but she had no choice but to follow Arthur as he approached the cliff. The noise of the waves grew louder, she could smell the salty air, and it even seemed that the sea breeze came right out of the picture and lifted the hair around her face, tickling her cheeks.

Arthur and his companion were soon joined by the other ten dogs who gambolled and frolicked along the clifftop above Weatherstone Bay, barking and yelping with delight.

Suddenly, from nowhere it seemed, a tall man dressed all in purple robes appeared beside Arthur. They embraced each other then stood apart.

The man was old, with a wrinkled face and long white hair and beard. It seemed the young Arthur grew older and more serious, and even the dogs stopped their prancing and games in this man's presence.

Despite his age and fragility, the old man seemed to fairly hum with energy. It was as though he were buzzing or throbbing – as though, Bella thought, he was tuned into some mysterious force, or plugged into his own electricity supply.

It's Merlin, she guessed. It's the wizard.

'Why so serious?' asked Arthur, but something in the way he spoke suggested he knew already.

'It is time,' said Merlin.

'Today? Now?'

'Yes. I did warn you . . . You are King now and must rule without my help. I am old, Arthur, and tired, so tired. I need a rest. I need to go.'

'I shall miss you. You know I still need you.'

'You will grow stronger without me. You will rule well. I have done my job and will only return when Britain truly needs me again.'

'And the dogs?'

'. . . will come with me.'

'Oh, Merlin. Must they? Must they all? The little Belle is my constant friend, my constant companion. And the pretty Lady Isabelle will be so distraught . . .'

Merlin didn't answer. He embraced Arthur and there were tears on both their cheeks. 'Am I to give way to sentimentality now?' said Merlin, and he shook his head. 'Farewell,' he whispered, and he began to walk away, the eleven dogs following closely behind.

They came to the outer walls of the garden, and here Merlin stopped and the golden dogs gathered round him in a circle, their bright eyes watching him intently. Then, even as Arabella stared, the dogs began to alter.

They were turning to stone.

Before her very eyes she saw their colour fade, the sheen disappear from their coats and their outlines harden as they became solidified and still; nothing but statues.

But no, not all!

The littlest one, the one Arthur called Belle, had not been included. Merlin held up his hand as if to give his permission for the dog to go,

and she turned and ran, leaping over the tufts of grass and flowers all the way back to Arthur. He saw her coming and, with open arms, gathered her up to his chest and buried his head in her fur.

Merlin turned and began to walk away. Bella watched his tall, straight back as he strode away across the hillside. She strained to see which way he would go, but already the colours were fading and she couldn't make out his figure against the green hills any more.

She looked back to see Arthur. Lady Isabelle was so pleased to have the dog, she knew she was; she was going to tie a ribbon round her neck . . . Oh, she wanted to see! She wanted to hear! But the picture was growing more and more weak and the sounds were fading. She reached out, trying to catch it back, but her hand groped nothing but air.

'Come back!' she cried. 'Merlin! Arthur!'

'Hey, hey, what's the matter?' said a voice close by her ear. A large hand grasped her arm. 'Something disturbed you, little girl?'

Arabella spun round, snatching her arm away instinctively.

It was Mr Boyle.

Bella fought to gain control of herself. She

remembered with difficulty where she was and who she was. 'Nothing, it was nothing,' she spluttered. She turned back to the tapestry but now it was only a lifeless smudge of greens and browns. 'I think I just . . .'

'Yes, I think so too,' said Mr Boyle. 'I know the feeling,' and he wiped his sweating forehead with a large grey handkerchief, which he then proferred to her.

Bella shook her head.

'Thank you. No. I'm fine. I'll go now.'

'What was it you thought you saw, little girl? Did I hear you say *Merlin*?'

'No, nothing. I felt faint, that's all.'

Mr Boyle grinned nastily at her, showing some unpleasant grey teeth. 'It's all the upset with your dear father,' he said, 'I do hope he's recovering . . .'

Bella managed to nod that he was.

'Good. Good. Until tonight, then.'

'B-b-bye,' Bella stammered, so anxious to be rid of him that she hardly knew what she was saying.

Mr Boyle went on up the stairs slowly and heavily, and Bella ran quickly back down.

What a horrible man, she thought. Horrid, horrid! And what did he mean, 'until tonight'? She hadn't liked the sneaky expression in his goggle eyes when he'd said that, not at all.

Chapter Nineteen

Later that evening, Bella tried to explain to Billy what had happened with the tapestry.

'I suppose it's your mother,' said Billy, sadly.

'What is?'

'The vivid imagination. It must be inherited from her, since she's a writer and everything.'

'Don't you believe me?'

' 'Course I do! I wish I didn't. I just wish things like that happened to me. It's not fair, I've lived here all my life and I don't get all these exciting things happening to me.'

'I can't help it, Billy. I've always felt somehow *connected* to this place and now I think I know why. That must be why I knew there'd been a fountain in the courtyard and how I knew the way home. I don't understand how, Billy, but I *was* Lady Isabelle.'

'Didn't I look just a little bit like Arthur?' asked Billy, hopefully.

Arabella shook her head.

'Sorry.'

'Have you told your father?'

'Sort of. He was very excited at first, but then he said it wasn't proof although he did believe me. Now he can't even have another go at digging for the missing dog. If it wasn't turned to stone then it won't be buried, will it?'

'But what *did* happen to it? You ought to know, Bella, if you were really there. Did it stay like a normal dog? Did it turn to stone later? Did it . . .'

'Stop! Billy, I don't know! I knew when I was watching the picture but now I don't. I didn't even see where Merlin went to – or how the stone dogs got buried – nothing really useful! The only thing I learnt from it all is that the eleventh dog got away – and that it was called Belle, of course. I knew I knew that, but I just couldn't remember it.'

'So we're back to where we were before,' said Billy. 'We need a stand-in, a girl, to make them eleven again and bring them to life.'

'It seems so.'

'Would you dare do it?'

'Of course . . . but Daddy said not to. He said it was dangerous.'

'He's right. We mustn't, but oh, Bella, we seem so close I wish we could try! This is the first and only time in my life that I've wished I'd been born a girl!'

It was late that night when Arabella woke.

She listened intently; it was that deep, quieter-than-quiet silence which told her it was the middle of the night. What had woken her?

She strained her ears – yes, there was a sound, a footfall, clothes brushing against the wall.

Bella sat upright. She couldn't see anything as the bed curtains were drawn tight. She didn't dare open them. The sounds were closer – there was someone or something in her room.

'Dad? Billy?'

Suddenly the curtains were snatched open, two figures loomed in at her and, catching her kicking legs and arms in an iron-like grip, lifted her out of her bed. Before she had time to cry out, they bundled her straight up in a blanket, and thrust her into a sack. Then she felt herself being carried away down the stairs and into the garden.

Bella was bumped and swung about like an old sack of potatoes, but she was so tightly wrapped up, her arms wedged to her side and the blanket wrapped close over her face, that she could hardly even struggle, let alone shout for help. Tears of frustration and fear stung her eyes.

Of course it's Boyle and McGregor, she thought. But what did they want with her now? Why were they kidnapping her? Would they hold her to ransom? Anything, she supposed, to get at what her father knew.

At last the bumping stopped and the men upended the sack, tipping Bella out on to the damp grass beside the ten stone dogs. She wrestled with the blanket, pulling herself free from it at last, and sat up and looked around.

The lanterns were lit again, making the stone dogs look golden and magical. Behind them the shadows were black and deep but Bella was determined not to be frightened. The stone dogs stared down at her, and Bella drew a strange comfort from their kind faces. They

were her friends. She had known them. They would help her.

She turned to look at Mr Boyle.

He looked revolting.

His face was a wet, shiny mass of grey scales. His eyes, more bulbous than ever, without eyelash or eyebrow, were focused coldly on her.

'Take a good look, little girl,' he said nastily. 'Do you like it? You won't see anything like this again, I can promise you that. Curse that Egyptian magic!'

'Revolting,' she said, shrinking back from the hideous face and the stench of rotten fish which blasted from his mouth in a thick cloud. She shivered, gathering up the blanket around her. 'What do you want? Why did you bring me here?'

'We've got such a lovely plan for you,' said

Darren McGregor, shuffling up close so Bella could smell his damp, musty smell. 'Oh, it'll make your hair curl, it will. Hee, hee, make your hair *grow* more like, yes, all over, and your ears and your teeth!'

'All right, McGregor!' warned Boyle.

Bella stared at them, beginning to understand . . .

'You can't!' she cried. 'You can't!'

'No, no, dear girl,' soothed Mr Boyle, taking her firmly by the arm in an iron grip. 'Don't take on so. It is not I who *can't*, but your father who *wouldn't*.'

'So you found out about the diary? You read the inscription?' asked Bella. 'How? How do you always do it?'

'Never you mind. There are ways and means,' said Boyle, leaning close. He smiled and a snake's forked tongue slithered out from between his lips, quivering and trembling, almost touching her cheek . . .

Bella screamed.

Boyle and McGregor laughed.

'There's more to me than meets the eye,' said Boyle.

'And less, on some occasions,' added McGregor, grinning.

'Now, come on. Let's get on with this,' said Boyle. He still held her arm firmly, and now he pulled her roughly over to sit between the stone dogs. 'Somehow,' he said, 'somehow, I think you'll be more than suitable for this job . . . Arabella!'

McGregor held Bella in place while Mr Boyle returned to the centre of the circle. His face, Bella noticed, was changing all the time; now feathers coated the back of his head like a strange hat and his fingers and arms were downy with feathers too. Boyle twitched his arms angrily, as if trying to shake them off.

'Blast it!' he cried. 'Not now! Not now!' He closed his eyes and, with an enormous effort and cry of pain, he managed to bring his arms back to normal. 'It's getting worse,' he muttered. 'Much worse.'

'Hurry up!' urged McGregor.

Mr Boyle threw him a dark look.

'Thank you, McGregor,' he said. Then, taking a deep breath, he began to recite his version of the ancient rhyme he had overheard Bradberry read from Archibald Gumm's diary.

'Gold-hunters, ten in number,
Granite cold they rest and slumber.

For revival, complete the pack.
With maiden I shall bring them back!'

He reached out and touched the first dog, calling it by name, then went on round the whole circle, touching and naming each one. Finally, when he reached Bella, he rested his cold hand firmly on her head and, keeping it there, said in a deep, slow, voice:

'The eleventh. *Belle . . !* Come awake, Belle! Come!'

Arabella flinched. She looked up at his mad, gleaming eyes. He knew! He knew the missing dog's name! Had he seen the moving picture too? Was nothing safe from this terrible man?

'At last you're here. At last we have eleven. Come, Belle, and join the pack. Come, all you Weatherstone dogs. Come BACK TO LIFE!'

Chapter Twenty

Billy had a strange dream.

It began with the sound of his door creaking open and then, so distinctly, the pitter-patter of an animal's feet on the polished floorboards. Lady, he thought. He sat up. In the dim light at the doorway a dog was standing.

'Lady,' he whispered, and the dog trotted over to him. He reached out his hand, but when he stroked its head it was cold to touch and rough, like sandpaper. Alarmed, but horribly fascinated, his fingers traced its eyes and nose and stroked its ears until at last he knew for certain, and he snatched his hand away and scrambled back across the bed.

The dog was made of stone.

Then, he supposed, he must have woken up. But he didn't remember opening his eyes or anything in the dream changing. He was on the edge of the bed, crouching against the wall, the bedroom door was open and the feel of the gritty stone still lingered in his fingers . . .

I never have dreams like that, Billy thought. I must be catching something from Bella. Stone dogs. Bella. *Boyle*, whirred his confused brain.

Something was wrong.

He jumped out of bed and hurried downstairs. Bella's bedroom door was open, her bed was empty.

In the loo? No, the light hadn't been on. Gone out? Then why hadn't she told him?

He went to the window. Yes, the lights again! It must be Boyle and McGregor, but what about Bella? Had she followed them? Why hadn't she told him? He was really worried now and, dashing out of the room, he flung himself down the stairs two at a time and out into the garden.

Billy ran until he reached the end of the orchard, then he stopped and went more slowly and carefully into the part where the stone dogs were.

He was right: there was Mr Boyle, horrid Mr Boyle with his damp fish lips and goggle eyes. And there was poor Bella, held down by McGregor and shivering so much Billy could see her pyjamas tremble.

What could he do?

Mr Boyle was calling the dogs' names and reciting the rhyme Mr Bradberry had found only that day. How did the beast know it? Billy stared at him, fascinated. Always one step ahead, thought Billy, just like Bella had said.

'It's worked!' cried Boyle, throwing up his arms and letting out an enormous shriek of glee. 'Look! Look!'

Billy looked.

His heart stopped beating. His mouth dropped open.

Everything was different. Right before his very eyes he saw the dogs were beginning to move and change. Now they were glowing with colour, no longer grey but brown and golden, and they were moving, shaking themselves, licking themselves . . .

The magic had worked.

Billy looked again at the spot where only moments ago Bella had been. Bella had disappeared, and now, in her place, standing on all fours, tail wagging, was a small golden-haired dog – the eleventh member of Merlin's magic circle.

The moment Boyle had begun to recite the rhyme, Bella had known it was going to work. It was as if a door were opening and someone was saying, 'Come in. Welcome.' It reminded her of the time she'd had a tooth out under gas. The gas had seemed to come out of the tube and suck her away, gently, invitingly, into a deep, deep sleep. She was wide awake now, but there was the same tingling feeling in her fingers and toes and she felt light-headed.

She watched Mr Boyle, no longer afraid of him, and when she heard his voice it was as though it was coming down a funnel, echoing and reverberating.

She shifted on the grass. Her back felt awkward, as if she'd slept on it all twisted. She arched it, and it felt as though she were releasing a hidden spring – so comfortable like this. Her legs felt all wrong: she stretched them, re-arranged them. That was better. Her chin itched, so did her ears. She lifted her hand to scratch . . . but that wasn't her arm, it was her leg! She smiled. How odd, she thought, this is much easier and she scratched and scratched, her long nails combing through her fur wonderfully well. Why didn't I ever do this before? she wondered, and put out her tongue to lick her cold nose.

Then she understood. She knew it before the words could form in her mind. She smelt dog, she felt dog, she *was* a dog. They let me in, she thought. I've done the

magic. I've broken the spell, and she felt intense excitement and joy.

Strong, wild smells filled her nostrils – new, exhilarating smells. Around her the other ten dogs barked and yelped as they were released from their stone shapes. They were glad to be free and their enthusiasm was catching. She stamped her paws, wiggled her bottom and wagged her tail. She was a dog. She was one of Merlin's dogs and it was marvellous!

She saw Mr McGregor staring at her with a strange, almost apologetic expression on his weaselly face. She opened her mouth to call to him and instead a volley of high-pitched barks rang out.

'It worked,' said McGregor. 'You've really gone and done it now, boss. This could be quite bad . . .'

'Shut up you idiot. No use getting cold feet now. You didn't think I could do it, did you?'

'Not really,' McGregor admitted. 'Still, she doesn't look unhappy, does she?'

'Which one is she?' asked Boyle, peering down at the seething mass of hairy bodies. 'I've lost her.'

'Don't know now. They all look the same. I wonder what it's like . . .'

Their words didn't mean much to Bella. Soon their voices were nothing to her at all; she heard them but it was as if they were speaking a different language, familiar but making no sense. It was to the other dogs that she listened: like tuning in to a new radio station, gradually she began to understand them, although no words were ever spoken.

The dogs were milling around, sniffing the grass, each other, everything. Shyly, Arabella joined in with them. They began nuzzling, smelling, licking and soon she did the same to them. At the back of her human mind she remembered how it had been when she'd joined the longed-for first division of the netball team. It was like that only better, as though she'd just scored the winning goal for them too.

And the energy! There was so much mischievous energy running through them they couldn't keep still. They rocked and bumped each other, intertwining their supple bodies, weaving around as if moved by invisible currents. They were anxious to be off, to be running. Bella could sense the need to go – she felt it too in her legs and toes. Run, run!

Mr Boyle was shouting. What was he trying to say? Bella tried to understand the words coming from his mouth, sensing they were important. Was he sending them out to find something? A stick? A bone? But it wasn't important. *He* wasn't important, they all knew that. Leaving Mr Boyle, arms waving and mouth moving angrily with the unknown words, the dogs, with a sudden surge forward and flurry of barking, formed into a tight pack and rushed away like one animal into the surrounding darkness.

Whooping, yelping and barking with delight, Arabella raced away with her friends.

Across the night air she caught new noises

and new smells. It was as if she'd been given six noses, all different, each one tuned in to a particular type of smell. Smell became dimensional, giving clear colour pictures of rabbits and horse manure and badgers and mice. Her nose could see! And her feet! Like running barefoot but without the fear of treading on glass or stones, because these feet were tough and never made mistakes.

It was dark but her dog's eyes saw everything she needed to see and what she couldn't see she could smell.

The soft earth squelched between her toes, the grass slithered, flowers erupted in scent as she trod them down. The air whistled through her fur, streamed her ears flat on her head and pulled out her tail like a banner flying behind her.

There was less and less of Bella the girl. Brilliant, brilliant, she had thought as they set off and now, as the pack tired of their race over the fields and hedges, Bella the dog's thoughts were wordless.

There was a change in the dogs' rhythm. Moving as one, turning like a shoal of fish, they headed back towards the house. Invisible, silent messages crossed the air between the dogs as together, in perfect harmony, they began to stride purposefully back over the grass.

'Here they come!' yelled Mr Boyle, jumping up from where he had been sitting waiting. 'Just a bit of high spirits, I should think. Now, let's round them up and get some ropes on them before they go off.'

'How, boss? There's too many of them and they don't listen to you. You were a bit hasty with this, weren't you? What's the plan now?'

'I told you, round them up . . . Hey, dogs, here! Here!'

'You said they'd accept you as boss because Merlin's gone, but it doesn't look like that to me.'

'Oh, doesn't it? What does it look like to you?'

'There they go,' said Mr McGregor, ignoring Boyle. 'They went straight past!'

'Well, don't just stand there! Follow them!' roared Mr Boyle.

The eleven dogs, eyes shining, ears erect, had trotted purposefully past the two men and now went on to an outcrop of stones above the bay. Here at last they paused, sniffing and examining the grass. Finally, after much consideration, one of the dogs began to dig.

'He's digging!' roared McGregor as he and Boyle drew near. He raised the lantern. 'Look!'

'I can see.'

'What's he up to then?' asked McGregor. 'Looking for a bone?'

'What do you think he's looking for, idiot! What do Merlin's dogs look for? What is the whole point of this exercise, McGregor, but to get GOLD!'

'And is there some right here?'

'Well, the dogs think so.'

They fell silent, watching the dog scrabble and dig at the soft earth. A second also began and then a third so that the hole grew rapidly wider and deeper. Soon there was a large saucer-shaped hole and then, suddenly, the earth shifted and began to slip inwards, taking the dog with it.

The dog disappeared with a slither of earth and stone.

Boyle leant over and shone his lantern down into the hole.

'It's gone!' remarked McGregor.

'I can see that!' Mr Boyle stared, wondering. A second dog jumped into the crater and slithered down into the space, and then a third followed too.

Mr Boyle caught hold of one by its collar.

'Here, come back!' he said sharply. 'Stay! Here!'

But the dog froze at his touch, turned back its head and glared at Mr Boyle with its round brown eyes. Slowly, warningly, the skin around its muzzle lifted, showing pink gums and very sharp white teeth. Mr Boyle let go instantly. A low growl rumbled and throbbed in the dog's chest.

'Whoops!' Boyle kept his hands close to his sides as he knelt beside the growling dog. 'Er, Arabella?' he asked softly. 'Arabella, is it you?'

The dog didn't respond. It turned away from him and, with a flick of its tail, it jumped down the hole and disappeared. The other dogs followed until all had gone.

'Now what, boss?'

'We follow. Come on, look sharp and bring the lantern. You won't be able to see a thing.'

'What about you?'

'I am going to try . . .' Mr Boyle grunted loudly, '. . . if I can, to fly.'

McGregor looked at him sharply.

'Watch it, boss, you don't look too good.'

Boyle's face was sweaty and pale. One or two feathers sprouted around his ears but nothing else.

'Phew! It's getting worse, I can't do it. Better save my energy. I have a feeling I'm going to need all my resources down there! Come on!'

Chapter Twenty-One

The sky was now tinged with pale blue and pale purple with a hint of rose and yellow over by the rising sun.

Billy looked up in wonder. It was going to be a lovely day and Bella was going to miss it. That was all he could think about: that Bella was a dog, would have no interest in sunshine or boat-trips or, or anything . . . and he had done nothing to prevent it.

I didn't do anything, he thought. Nothing. I'm feeble. Simple-minded. I should have saved her. I should have rushed in and . . .

He sighed. He was so cold and stiff he could hardly think straight. He was damp and shivering uncontrollably.

Billy could still see Boyle and McGregor, but they had their backs to him; they wouldn't notice him now. As far as he could make out, watching from that distance, the dogs had all jumped down into the ground. Into a cave, he wondered? It looked like the two men would follow too.

He began to stretch his arms and flex his legs. There was only one thing to do – go back to Weatherstone Hall for reinforcements.

He wasn't frightened of being seen now and he ran towards the house, his bare feet slipping on the wet grass. We must get to Bella before anything too awful happens . . . Could anything be more awful? I don't know, I don't know, he answered himself. Just let me get help. Then he stopped dead in his tracks – but who? Who could he possibly get?

His mother? She'd be hopeless. She'd want to call the police and the fire brigade and . . . no good. Mr Bradberry would have been his first choice, but of course he was no good now because of his broken leg. Uncle Jack? But he was so old and fragile. He wouldn't be any good. There's only me, he thought feebly. OK, OK, he told himself, you will just have to do.

He sprinted onward again, this time skirting round to the back of the house where he grabbed his wellingtons and an old mac from the cloakroom. If they really had gone underground, which it looked like, he'd have to get his torch – there it was beside Uncle Jack's second-best bow and arrow . . . Billy hesitated. He was under strict instructions never to touch the bow and arrow, but . . . Guiltily he swung the quiver over his shoulder and picked up the large bow. It was all in a good cause. Uncle Jack would understand. Finally, he put a large ball of garden twine into his pocket. If he was really going down into the caves, he needed to be able to find his way back out again.

There was no sign of anyone by the time Billy reached the stony outcrop, but the mess of footprints and pawprints showed clearly in the freshly turned earth. Billy peered at the hole, shining his torch down. It was as he'd thought; the opening was in the roof of the tunnel. The floor was about three metres below.

Oh well, Billy thought, and jumped.

He landed safely on a heap of grass and soil which had fallen in from above. It was much warmer underground and very dark. Billy looked up at the light of the sky showing through the hole in the roof, then forwards into the pitch black. He was going to have to be very brave . . . He shone the torch round the tunnel. Now he could see that the walls and roof, all knotty from protruding roots and stones, had been strengthened with planks of wood so it was a man-made corridor he was in. He wondered who had built it and why.

Billy tied one end of his string to a large knobbly root and prepared to let the rest unwind slowly in his hand. He breathed in deeply – the air was musty and earthy, clogging his nostrils.

'Come along, Billy,' he said out loud. 'On we go.'

Apart from the soft noise of his own feet on the soil, there was no other sound as slowly, following the foot- and dog-prints in the earth, Billy advanced.

Somewhere far ahead the Weatherstone dogs ran onwards.

They didn't falter or hesitate. It was as if they were being drawn by an invisible string as they moved on through the underground passages, their keen senses of smell and hearing guiding them.

At last the dogs came to a large, dimly lit chamber.

The domed stone roof soared above them like a cathedral. Miniature holes in the rock roof and walls, like tiny windows, let in pinprick beams of light from the outside. The minuscule shafts of light criss-crossed the cave, glanced off the rocks and glistened on the wet walls.

Water trickled down the walls. Vast stalagmites rose from the ground like old black candles with hundreds of years of uneven wax on them. Pointed knobbly grey stalactites hung from the ceiling like dirty icicles. In some places the two had grown together and fused, forming gigantic, weirdly shaped pillars.

In the centre of this extraordinary cave, on an ornate stone table, was a glass coffin. In the coffin was the object which had drawn the eleven dogs down to this secret place –

Merlin.

The dogs clustered around the coffin, sniffing, hoping for a hint of Merlin's scent, but

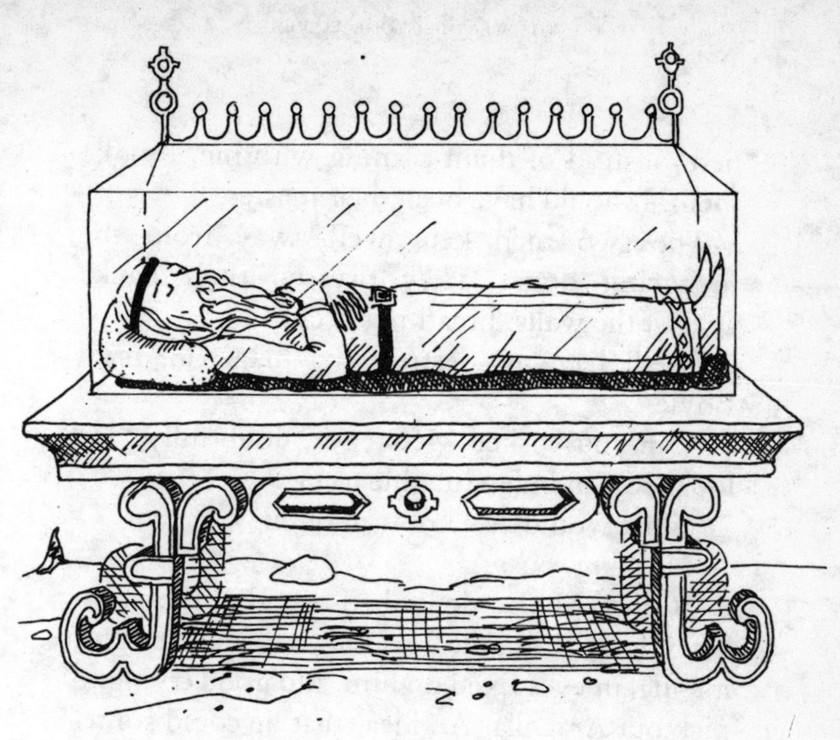

even as their noses twitched, the noise of their followers resounded in the vast chamber.

The dogs turned as one, all eyes on the two men. Like one animal of many parts, the dogs curled their lips in a snarl, their hackles rose on their shoulders and a threatening noise rattled in their chests.

'Yikes!' said McGregor nervously. 'Looks like they mean business. What's that in the glass box?'

'Merlin,' said Boyle. 'It's Merlin and his magic must be too strong. It's pulled the dogs here, instead of them coming with me. I woke them. I should have been their master.'

The two men kept well away from the menacing dogs. They pressed their backs against the walls, breathing deeply.

'We'll have to destroy the magician,' said Boyle.

'Can you?' asked McGregor, doubtfully. 'He looks sort of indestructible to me.'

'What would you know about it?'

'Nothing, boss.'

'Right.' Mr Boyle looked round at the dogs. They looked identical and all had their bright, intelligent eyes fixed on him. No good trying to pick out Arabella. An idea, that he could somehow use her to his advantage, died even as it occurred to him.

Arabella the dog stared back at Mr Boyle. She was so entirely a dog now that she didn't know this man's name or why she hated him, only that she did and must guard Merlin with her life. She was glad when his gaze swept over her.

Then, from somewhere deep inside the cliff, came a muffled cry: 'Ara-bella! Ara-bella!'

The voice triggered something inside the dog which was Bella and she trembled, quivered, as something stirred inside her.

'Did you hear anything?' asked McGregor, looking round, straining his ears.

'No.'

'I thought I did . . .'

'Ara-bella. Ara-bella.'

'There, didn't you hear it?' said McGregor again. He was beginning to feel worried. The whole place gave him the jitters. The dogs scared him and so did that old man in the glass box.

'You're imagining it,' said Boyle.

But he wasn't and that voice, whoever it came from, had had a deep effect on Bella. It was the beginning of a realization that she was not really a dog.

'Wh-what are we going to do?' asked McGregor.

"We're going to have to destroy him, but we'll never do it while those dogs are guarding the coffin like that . . .' Mr Boyle looked round the cave, searching for anything he might use to help. 'I have to get the dogs away, but how?'

Then his eyes fell on an old wooden torch stuck into an iron hoop on the wall. He looked from that to the dogs and back again.

All dogs hated fire. Even Merlin's dogs hated fire.

'You smoke, McGregor – give me your matches.'

Nervously, McGregor did as he was told. He kept one eye on the dogs all the time – he didn't like the way they watched him.

'I'm going to take the dogs out to the sea,' said Boyle. 'When I reach the cave entrance on the cliff, I'll force them over the edge. It's not a long swim to the beach and I'll follow them – in a rather more slippery shape! While I'm doing that, you destroy the coffin and the magician. The dogs will never obey me until he's gone. Use anything you can lay your hands on.'

'Like what?'

'Stones. Sticks. Your hands! Think, man, think! It's double the money for you.'

'And how will you get the dogs down the tunnel?' asked McGregor.

'Watch!'

A nasty smile spread across Mr Boyle's grey, sweaty face. He took the torch down from the wall and rearranged the old peat and moss inside it, then he set fire to it. In seconds the thing was an enormous flare, illuminating the chamber with ghastly dancing shadows and a vibrant red light.

Mr Boyle stepped forward, thrusting the flare towards the dogs.

The dogs cowered back.

They growled and showed their teeth, but all the time, as he advanced, the dogs moved backwards, away from the flames.

Back and back went the pack of dogs with Mr Boyle always in front, jabbing at them with his stick of fire, pushing them away, down towards a small tunnel far from the coffin.

'Ha, ha!' he cried. 'This is it! Now I shall have you for myself. Won't we have fun, little doggies, won't we have fun? The nasty deeds we can do. The treasures we can discover. The riches. The gold . . . the GOLD!'

Mr McGregor listened to the yelps, barks and shouts as they grew fainter and fainter. When they had quite gone, he felt very much alone. He didn't like this place and he didn't like this job, but he'd had worse. Opening up those old Egyptian tombs was worse, what with those old bodies all crumbling away in their wrappings. Yuk! This would be a piece of cake, wouldn't it?

He picked up a large, sharp stone and

approached the coffin. It didn't even look very strong, just glass . . .

He peered into the coffin and stared down at the old man. Was he alive or dead? He stared and stared. Was he breathing? Was there the slightest rise and fall of his chest?

McGregor jumped as a drop of water fell on to his head. He looked up; another drip landed on his nose. It was very cold. That's how these stalactites and stala-ma-thingies grow, he thought. Loads of drips, one on top of the other. Another drip splashed on to his head. He stepped sideways, closer to the coffin. Was there a flicker in the old man's face? Did he see the eyelids move? He scrutinized the body carefully.

Another drop fell on his head, and another. It was getting cold. McGregor was freezing, his whole head was cold and his neck. I wish this blinking dripping would stop, he thought, as more and more drops dashed on to his head.

He tried to raise his arm to smash the stone against the coffin, but he was too cold. He tried to move away from the coffin, but he was too numb; soon he was so cold and stiff that he couldn't move or think at all.

Chapter Twenty-Two

The dogs, yelping and barking, backed down the narrow tunnel that led to the sea. They were tightly bunched, twisting and turning, trying to get close enough to Boyle to bite, but always thrust back by the terrible burning torch.

Gradually, the air grew cooler and more and more salty. The roar of the sea beating against the rocks became louder as they turned a bend in the tunnel and came to a small, irregular-shaped cave which opened out directly on to the cliff face. Below them was the surging, swirling blue sea.

Mr Boyle laughed.

'Trapped!' he roared. 'You're trapped. You'll have to swim for it, dogs. Go on! Jump!'

The first dog was now on the very edge of the cliff. Its paws slithered and slipped on the stone, then suddenly it couldn't hold on any longer and over it went. It turned in mid-air and splashed safely into the water. Then it lifted its fine pointed nose and began swimming for land.

'Good, good,' said Boyle. 'Hurry, hurry!' he urged the next. If they all reached the shore before him, he might lose them again! Speed was all-important, but he dare not jump until they'd all gone in.

The next one jumped and then the next and all the time Mr Boyle poked at them with his flare, forcing them on.

Bella had been one of the first dogs to arrive there and instinctively had veered away from the mouth of the cave. Quite by luck, she found a crevice beside the entrance where she squashed herself to hide. It was out of the daylight and damp and here she began to try and sort out her strange thoughts and feelings.

Back in Merlin's chamber she had distinctly heard her name being called. Up until that moment, Bella hadn't known her name – she had become so much a dog that she was lost to the rest of the world. But that voice, calling her, had triggered something inside her, had woken something which was now trying to respond.

She watched Mr Boyle's face and tried to remember, tried to fight against the dogginess that was in and around her and threatening to engulf her yet again. She forced herself to think about the voice she'd heard and found she could hear it distinctly, as if she could play it back on a tape.

Arabella. Arabella. Arabella.

That was her. That was Arabella the girl, not a dog.

She looked again at Boyle and now, as she watched and listened to him, she understood what he was saying.

What am I doing? she thought. Did I dream about being a dog? Was this a dream? It felt like a dream, to understand human speech but be unable to speak, to still feel bent and small . . . She looked down and saw her feet—

They were hairy paws!

So it wasn't a dream, it was real! She

remembered with a sudden jolt how Boyle had forced her to join the circle of dogs and how wonderful it had been – at first. Now it felt all wrong; now she was a girl trapped inside a dog's body and it was wrong!

And if I don't get out, she thought, Boyle will win. While there are eleven dogs he can do terrible things, but if there are only ten again . . . he'll lose.

Arabella closed her eyes and began to focus her attention on her body. She concentrated on picturing her hands, her feet, her knees, her face, every part, willing it to return to what it should be.

All the time she kept a fraction of her mind on what was going on in the cave and was aware of the dogs passing her, splashing down into the sea below. I hope Boyle hasn't been counting, she thought – If he missed her . . . ! Oh, she dreaded to think what he might do.

She opened her eyes and stared hard at Boyle.

I am a girl, she told herself. I am a girl. You can't win, Boyle. I am a girl and so there are only ten dogs. I am a girl and your eleven is broken. I AM A GIRL!

She shivered with the cold. Her feet hurt; there were lots of tiny pebbles and bits of grit on the floor and her skin was wet. She wrapped her arms round her damp pyjamas and hugged herself . . .

Pyjamas? Arms? Skin!

She held her hand up in front of her face and wiggled her fingers. Fingers! She had a human hand again with real fingers! A smile spread across her face. The magic was broken.

Mr Boyle had lost.

'Go on! Go on!' Mr Boyle was roaring at the dogs. His flare was getting fainter, the peat was burning quickly and had almost gone. He had to get all the dogs into the sea before it went out. He poked and thrust at the final golden-haired dog as it hesitated on the edge of the cave then, finally, it too jumped.

Jubilantly, Mr Boyle flung his arms in the air and hopped around the cave.

'Done it! Done it!' he cried, then, at almost the same instant, his joy turned to amazement and horror.

'Hey!' he cried, staring down into the sea. 'What's happening? What the . . . '

Instead of leaping into the sea like the others, the last dog had changed. Right before Mr Boyle's very eyes, the dog had paled to grey, turned to stone, and plummeted like a rock into the water.

And now, looking down into the sea, Boyle scanned the choppy waves for the golden heads which should have been bobbing up and down as they swam to the shore. But there was nothing, no golden dogs.

The Weatherstone dogs, stone statues once more, had sunk and were lying on the sand at the bottom of the sea.

Mr Boyle remained motionless beside the cave mouth for several moments. He was breathing deeply. Bella, watching from her hideout, saw the rise and fall of his chest, saw how still he was and wondered whether she might dare to creep out. But just as she was about to make a move, he turned round.

His face was contorted and twisted. His cheeks were green and his throat yellow. His eyes were slits and nothing remained of his nose except his nostrils. A black flickering snake's tongue darted out of his mouth as he roared, 'Arabella, you have tricked me!'

So he had guessed.

Arabella trembled in her hiding place, squeezing herself back into the darkness, but she knew it wasn't any good. There was nowhere to hide.

Mr Boyle stamped back into the cave and began looking for her. It was only seconds before he found her and, grabbing her by the arm, he pulled her out into the daylight.

'So, you undid the magic, did you?' The snake's tongue quivered at her. 'Decided to stop my bit of fun? Well, things aren't as easy as that, my dear girl. I don't give up so soon, oh no!' He began to drag her back along the corridor towards Merlin's chamber. 'Come on, come on,' he said. 'This is not over yet. I was close, very close and I shall succeed. Nothing will stop me. I want Merlin's Eleven and I shall have them.'

'You'll never get them,' said Bella. 'Why don't you give up now?'

She wanted to add that he looked pretty sick,

too, but didn't dare. Boyle's snake face had twisted and slithered back into a human shape, but he looked grey and sweaty and he seemed to find breathing difficult.

They reached Merlin's chamber at last.

'McGregor! McGREGOR!' shouted Boyle, but his voice just echoed round the great cave. There was no sign of McGregor.

Boyle pulled Bella across to the glass coffin where Merlin still lay peacefully. A large pointed stone rested on top of the coffin.

'Where is he? Where is the silly little idiot?' hissed Boyle.

Bella was staring at the stalagmite beside the coffin. She was quite certain it hadn't been there before and it was such a strange shape – sort of human.

'OH!' The truth suddenly dawned on her.

'What is it?'

'McGregor's here. That's him,' she said, pointing to the grey, waxy-looking growth on the floor. 'Or that *was* him. Poor chap.'

Boyle stared at the stalagmite and prodded it with his finger. He peered at it. It was McGregor, there was no doubt about it. He could see where his face had been and even his arm where he had been about to strike the coffin with the stone.

'Dang and blast!' he said. 'I'll have to do it myself.'

He picked up the stone and raised it high above his head.

'Stop or I'll shoot!' a voice cried from the back of the cave.

Boyle and Bella spun round.

Walking towards them was Billy, bow and arrow poised to shoot.

Chapter Twenty-Three

Mr Boyle burst out laughing. He threw back his head, almost choking himself with his laughter. His loud guffaws resounded round and round the echoing chamber.

'You! A boy! Ha, ha, ha!'

'I'm serious,' said Billy, and he did look it with his small white face set hard and solemn. 'You must let go of Bella. Let her come to me.'

'Don't be daft!' snapped Boyle. 'I need her.'

'I'm no use now the dogs are at the bottom of the sea,' said Bella. 'What good am I . . . ?'

'I can still get them. We can raise them again. Oh, the gold, think of the gold. Gold beneath the soil, coins dropped, rings flung off in a passion, treasure chests buried by pirates – doubloons and sovereigns and gold crowns sunk at sea in storms . . . All that gold will belong to me! We will find it together, you and I . . . '

'I won't help!' cried Bella.

'You will!'

'I won't. Let me go!' She pulled and tugged, but his grip was firm.

'This is your last warning,' said Billy, and he pulled the arrow back even tighter against the bow.

'You can't shoot that thing,' said Boyle, but he sounded worried now. 'You wouldn't dare . . .'

'One . . . two . . . three!'

Billy fired. The arrow shot across the cave and caught Mr Boyle in the leg. He screamed, let go of Bella and toppled on to the ground.

Billy dropped his weapon and rushed over to them.

'Sorry! Sorry, Mr Boyle,' he said. 'Oh dear, I didn't really mean to do it, only you wouldn't let her go and I said I would and . . . Oh dear, are you all right?'

'No, no!' shrieked Mr Boyle. 'Of course I'm not! Help me up. Help me!'

But the children couldn't touch him. They only took a step back from him as he lay writhing on the floor, watching him, staring at him.

'There's no blood,' said Billy, in awe. 'Look, no blood.'

Mr Boyle had pulled up his trouser leg and, as Billy said, there wasn't any blood around the wound at all.

'Help me!' cried Boyle.

But Bella and Billy couldn't move.

Mr Boyle's skin was changing: he was altering form again.

'I won't! I won't!' cried Mr Boyle. 'Not now!' He struggled, trying to get up off the floor. 'I won't let this happen – stop this happening!'

'What is it?' asked Bella.

'The fish. The fish is coming.'

'Oh,' said Bella. 'This isn't the right place for it at all.'

'Help me!'

Mr Boyle looked down at his leg. It seemed the arrow had triggered off the animal change and now silvery scales were creeping over the surface of his skin. His trousers seemed to melt into his legs as his feet began to disappear, began to merge together into a purplish grey fin. His hands were shrinking, receding backwards up into his arm. Then his arm seemed to be sucked up into his shoulder and his fingers were growing long and spiny until they weren't fingers any more but spines of a fin protruding from his shoulder. The rest of his clothes were absorbed into his body as if they were melted into his new, silver skin.

'It shouldn't happen here, not now!' said Boyle. 'Why is it happening? Why?'

'Can't you get yourself back?' asked Bella, timidly. 'You did before.'

'No, no, it's too difficult. I can't! It's coming on its own. Ow, ow, my face, my head!'

Mr Boyle's face was stretched and distorted as his mouth suddenly widened, growing purple lips and sharp teeth. His hair had gone, his whole head gleamed with a silvery, slithery-smooth sheen. His eyes bulged, and grew black and wet, the eyebrows disappeared. Huge gill flaps emerged on either side of his head and began opening and closing, slowly, desperately.

'He can't breathe,' said Bella.

'Fish suffocate out of water,' said Billy.

'How horrid.'

'It does serve him right though.'

'He'll never get back again, will he? He's going to die.'

'Look!'

Drops of water were beginning to fall from the ceiling above. They fell with deadly accuracy on to the fish. Drip. Drip. Drop. And as they fell, they began to alter the fish. It began to change, just like Mr McGregor, into a grey, indistinct shape like one of the many others in the cave.

Bella and Billy stared spellbound for several minutes, then Bella said, 'There are lots and lots of stalagmites here. All odd shapes. Do you think . . .'

'All the people who have tried to get Merlin?' Billy suggested. 'That's what I was wondering.' He stared at what remained of Mr Boyle. 'I almost feel sorry for him, poor man. What a horrible way to go.'

'It serves him right,' Bella said. 'It pays him back for stealing from that Egyptian tomb he talked about and knocking over my dad.'

'I suppose you're right.'

'Come on, I think we'd better go.' Bella looked up at the dripping roof anxiously. 'I'd hate one of those drips to land on me.'

'What about Merlin?' asked Billy.

They went over the glass coffin and peered in at the sleeping figure of the old magician. His face was peaceful and grave. His breathing was almost impossible to see, so slight was the rise and fall of his chest, just like the breathing of a new baby.

'What a wonderful face. I wish we could take him out just for Dad to see . . . Or bring Dad here. He hasn't moved. I don't think any of us was important enough to wake him,' said Bella. 'Oh, look!'

As Bella had spoken, the tiniest fraction of a smile had crossed Merlin's face.

'Did you see? Did you see that?' she gasped.

Billy shook his head.

'He smiled. I'm sure he smiled. Oh, Billy, I think he smiled at *me*!'

*

There was the most enormous uproar the following day when it was found that Mr Boyle, Mr McGregor and the stone dogs had all disappeared. Bella had meant to tell her father exactly what had happened but when it came to it, she couldn't. She knew that if she did, her father would try and find Merlin's cave and she knew that if he succeeded, he stood a chance of being turned into a stony, candle-like stalagmite just like all the others. Merlin had no intention of being found by anyone.

'Now the dogs have gone, I suppose this means all your research is wasted,' said Bella, sadly. 'What will you do now?'

'Wasted? Goodness no!' roared her father. 'There are lots of papers here for me to go through and I won't give up on my quest for Merlin. He's around here somewhere, I'm absolutely certain. Do you know, last night I had the strangest dream?'

'Really?'

'Extraordinary,' said Mr Bradberry. 'I dreamt you'd been turned into a dog – I suppose I must have been thinking about that old rhyme again – and you'd gone down some long underground tunnel looking for Merlin's grave, and I was searching for you, trying to catch you, and

I was calling your name. I called it so loud I woke myself up. Funny, isn't it?'

'Very,' Bella agreed.

'I wonder what Boyle did with those dogs?' pondered Mr Bradberry. 'I do wish I wasn't stuck here in this room with my broken leg! Such an inconvenience!'

Secretly, Bella was very glad her father was immobilized – that way he was safe, for now anyway.

Later that day, Bella and Billy walked out in the sunshine to the clifftops and sat down on the springy grass, looking out across the turquoise sea below.

'I wonder if anyone will ever find the stone dogs again?' said Bella. 'I hate to think of them lying at the bottom of the sea like that with seaweed and whelks and things growing on them.'

'They won't know anything about it.'

'You're so practical! Look, there's Lady coming to join us. She's such a lovely dog . . . You know, Billy, it was really the most brilliant thing being a dog like that, because I wasn't pretending or anything, and every bit of me was dog – everything! There was one point, when I was in Merlin's chamber, when I was so lost in it all that I might never have come back.'

'You mean stayed a dog for ever?'

'Yes, for ever and ever . . . only I heard you calling me, calling my name, and that brought me back.'

'I didn't call your name,' said Billy, looking surprised. 'I didn't dare make any noise at all. I was creeping along, unravelling my string, guided by the noise you lot were making.'

'But I heard you call my name. I heard you.'

'Not me. It wasn't me, Bella, I swear!'

Bella frowned. 'Then it must have . . . it couldn't have . . . Oh, it doesn't matter anyway, but Daddy said he called my name in his sleep. Do you think . . . ?'

'I'd believe anything,' said Billy. 'Anything at all.'

Arabella grinned. 'You have to, don't you? What a strange, exciting night it was. Do you know, looking at Lady now, though I never thought it before, doesn't she look rather like the stone dogs?'

'Well, I suppose she does in a way, though she's black of course and smaller.' Billy sat upright, staring at the little dog. 'What is she up to over there? Digging?'

'Let's go and see.'

'Lady! Lady!' they called.

The black dog stopped scrabbling in the soil and looked round at them, wagging her tail. She backed off from the hole and sat down, obviously pleased with herself.

'What is it, Lady? What have you found?'

'OH! Golly, Bella, look!'

The children dropped to their knees beside the shallow hole Lady had scooped out and there, still half-buried and covered in soil, lay an old wooden box. Its brass straps and lock were green with tarnish and the wood had rotted and crumbled so parts of it were nothing but dust mingled with the earth. They pushed aside the soil and fragments of wood and there, inside the chest, was a heap of gold coins.

'Billy!'

'Oh, my! Oh, my golly gosh!' Billy gasped. 'We're rich! It's gold! It's buried treasure. It's like people find in books!'

'Yes, Billy, it is. But Billy, Lady found it.'

'So, do you want me to give it to her?'

'Silly, no! Look at her, Billy, look at her face!' said Arabella. 'Don't you see? She's a direct descendant of the dog before her and the one before that and the one before that. Why didn't I think of it before? That's why she likes me so much because, though I don't understand how I was here once. Remember that Merlin let Arthur have little Belle to keep, and Belle was a magic, gold-finding dog. If they always, right from then, kept one dog from each generation . . . Billy, your little Lady is directly related to the Weatherstone Eleven! She's proved it by finding this gold.'

'Oh, Bella, do you really think so?'

They stared at Lady.

But Lady only wagged her tail and licked her nose and that could have meant anything at all.

THE END